Hurtling Wings

SELECTED FICTION WORKS BY
L. RON HUBBARD

FANTASY
The Case of the Friendly Corpse
Death's Deputy
Fear
The Ghoul
The Indigestible Triton
Slaves of Sleep & The Masters of Sleep
Typewriter in the Sky
The Ultimate Adventure

SCIENCE FICTION
Battlefield Earth
The Conquest of Space
The End Is Not Yet
Final Blackout
The Kilkenny Cats
The Kingslayer
The Mission Earth Dekalogy*
Ole Doc Methuselah
To the Stars

ADVENTURE
The Hell Job series

WESTERN
Buckskin Brigades
Empty Saddles
Guns of Mark Jardine
Hot Lead Payoff

A full list of L. Ron Hubbard's
novellas and short stories is provided at the back.

*Dekalogy—a group of ten volumes

L. RON HUBBARD

Hurtling Wings

GALAXY
PRESS

Published by
Galaxy Press, LLC
7051 Hollywood Boulevard, Suite 200
Hollywood, CA 90028

Printed in the United States of America.

ISBN-10 1-59212-285-X
ISBN-13 978-1-59212-285-1

Library of Congress Control Number: 2007928447

Contents

Stories from *Pulp Fiction's* Golden Age

A ND it *was* a golden age.

The 1930s and 1940s were a vibrant, seminal time for a gigantic audience of eager readers, probably the largest per capita audience of readers in American history. The magazine racks were chock-full of publications with ragged trims, garish cover art, cheap brown pulp paper, low cover prices—and the most excitement you could hold in your hands.

"Pulp" magazines, named for their rough-cut, pulpwood paper, were a vehicle for more amazing tales than Scheherazade could have told in a million and one nights. Set apart from higher-class "slick" magazines, printed on fancy glossy paper with quality artwork and superior production values, the pulps were for the "rest of us," adventure story after adventure story for people who liked to *read*. Pulp fiction authors were no-holds-barred entertainers—real storytellers. They were more interested in a thrilling plot twist, a horrific villain or a white-knuckle adventure than they were in lavish prose or convoluted metaphors.

The sheer volume of tales released during this wondrous golden age remains unmatched in any other period of literary history—hundreds of thousands of published stories in over nine hundred different magazines. Some titles lasted only an issue or two; many magazines succumbed to paper shortages during World War II, while others endured for decades yet. Pulp fiction remains as a treasure trove of stories you can read, stories you can love, stories you can remember. The stories were driven by plot and character, with grand heroes, terrible villains, beautiful damsels (often in distress), diabolical plots, amazing places, breathless romances. The readers wanted to be taken beyond the mundane, to live adventures far removed from their ordinary lives—and the pulps rarely failed to deliver.

In that regard, pulp fiction stands in the tradition of all memorable literature. For as history has shown, good stories are much more than fancy prose. William Shakespeare, Charles Dickens, Jules Verne, Alexandre Dumas—many of the greatest literary figures wrote their fiction for the readers, not simply literary colleagues and academic admirers. And writers for pulp magazines were no exception. These publications reached an audience that dwarfed the circulations of today's short story magazines. Issues of the pulps were scooped up and read by over thirty million avid readers each month.

Because pulp fiction writers were often paid no more than a cent a word, they had to become prolific or starve. They also had to write aggressively. As Richard Kyle, publisher and editor of *Argosy*, the first and most long-lived of the pulps, so pointedly explained: "The pulp magazine writers, the best of them, worked for markets that did not write for critics or attempt to satisfy timid advertisers. Not having to answer to anyone other than their readers, they wrote about human beings on the edges of the unknown, in those new lands the future would explore. They wrote for what we would become, not for what we had already been."

Some of the more lasting names that graced the pulps include H. P. Lovecraft, Edgar Rice Burroughs, Robert E. Howard, Max Brand, Louis L'Amour, Elmore Leonard, Dashiell Hammett, Raymond Chandler, Erle Stanley Gardner, John D. MacDonald, Ray Bradbury, Isaac Asimov, Robert Heinlein—and, of course, L. Ron Hubbard.

In a word, he was among the most prolific and popular writers of the era. He was also the most enduring—hence this series—and certainly among the most legendary. It all began only months after he first tried his hand at fiction, with L. Ron Hubbard tales appearing in *Thrilling Adventures, Argosy, Five-Novels Monthly, Detective Fiction Weekly, Top-Notch, Texas Ranger, War Birds, Western Stories,* even *Romantic Range.* He could write on any subject, in any genre, from jungle explorers to deep-sea divers, from G-men and gangsters, cowboys and flying aces to mountain climbers, hard-boiled detectives and spies. But he really began to shine when he turned his talent to science fiction and fantasy of which he authored nearly fifty novels or novelettes to forever change the shape of those genres.

Following in the tradition of such famed authors as Herman Melville, Mark Twain, Jack London and Ernest Hemingway, Ron Hubbard actually lived adventures that his own characters would have admired—as an ethnologist among primitive tribes, as prospector and engineer in hostile climes, as a captain of vessels on four oceans. He even wrote a series of articles for *Argosy,* called "Hell Job," in which he lived and told of the most dangerous professions a man could put his hand to.

Finally, and just for good measure, he was also an accomplished photographer, artist, filmmaker, musician and educator. But he was first and foremost a *writer,* and that's the L. Ron Hubbard we come to know through the pages of this volume.

This library of Stories from the Golden Age presents the best of L. Ron Hubbard's fiction from the heyday of storytelling, the Golden Age of the pulp magazines. In these eighty volumes, readers are treated to a full banquet of 153 stories, a kaleidoscope of tales representing every imaginable genre: science fiction, fantasy, western, mystery, thriller, horror, even romance—action of all kinds and in all places.

Because the pulps themselves were printed on such inexpensive paper with high acid content, issues were not meant to endure. As the years go by, the original issues of every pulp from *Argosy* through *Zeppelin Stories* continue crumbling into brittle, brown dust. This library preserves the L. Ron Hubbard tales from that era, presented with a distinctive look that brings back the nostalgic flavor of those times.

L. Ron Hubbard's Stories from the Golden Age has something for every taste, every reader. These tales will return you to a time when fiction was good clean entertainment and the most fun a kid could have on a rainy afternoon or the best thing an adult could enjoy after a long day at work. Pick up a volume, and remember what reading is supposed to be all about. Remember curling up with a *great story*.

—Kevin J. Anderson

KEVIN J. ANDERSON *is the author of more than ninety critically acclaimed works of speculative fiction, including The Saga of Seven Suns, the continuation of the Dune Chronicles with Brian Herbert, and his* New York Times *bestselling novelization of L. Ron Hubbard's* Ai! Pedrito!

xi

Hurtling Wings

CHAPTER ONE

The Crash

THREE hundred miles an hour is too fast for anybody," said Georgia Kyle positively, but Cal only poised for the briefest instant on the catwalk of his racing plane to answer.

"Somebody will do it and it might as well be yours truly." With that, he lowered himself into his pit and pulled his goggles down over his forehead.

The girl's long black lashes dropped uncertainly down over her eyes, her face startlingly white under the jet of her hair. She looked up again and saw the picture Cal Bradley made sitting there in the narrow confines of his "office." She saw his striped helmet, his brown leather jacket, his frank blue eyes and his rugged face—the face of a man born to take chances.

Georgia laid her hand on the cowling. "Cal, I wish you'd listen to me just once. I've a feeling that—"

Cal Bradley paused in his perusal of the sky and the hundreds of ships lined up on the tarmacs of the great hangars. Puzzled, he looked down.

"Maybe it's silly," she went on, "and I know you'll laugh, but I have a premonition that you're going to crash today."

"The first day of the meet?" True to her prophecy, Cal laughed. "You've just got a case of jitters, honey. I'm going to live through this meet and a good many more. In fact, I'm going to live long enough to buy out your dad and marry you and win a thousand races. Maybe this ship is all I've got in the world, but it's enough. Now, if you don't look out, I'll blast the engine and blow you clean through the grandstand!"

Georgia laughed and backed away, almost bumping into her father, Speed Kyle, who was hobbling up in time to wish Cal luck.

"Be careful!" Georgia called, above the growing roar of the engine.

"Good luck, Cal!" shouted Speed, and with a beaming smile on his weather-beaten face, he watched the small but speedy racing plane taxi away toward the line.

When the dust had settled from Cal's prop wash, Speed turned to his daughter with pretended ferocity. "The idea, telling that youngster to be careful, just when he's out to make the record!"

"He can be careful and fly fast, too, can't he?"

"Humph!" Speed grunted, and took her arm, leading her away toward the grandstand. "There's not so much difference between auto racing and plane racing, Georgia, and there's no difference at all between the fellows that do the driving. Why, as old as I am, I'd give my eye teeth to be up there in one of the Kyle racers giving Cal Bradley the run of his young life."

"You aren't so old, Dad," said Georgia.

"No? Well, I'm the deuce of a lot older than I care to be. I was in the auto racing game in 1902, and I've been building airplanes for fourteen years."

Having heard the story since the days of her hair ribbons,

4

Georgia diverted her attention to the line where three ships were coming in side by side.

"All ready to go," she said. "I hope Cal doesn't turn the pylons too fast."

Speed's grunt was interrupted by the grinding voice through the microphones saying that Cal Bradley, Bill Conklin and Smoke Gregory, the three speed kings of the air, were about to race against each other and the record, and that this was the first of a series of high-speed events which would be held at the National Air Meet.

Speed looked at Conklin's ship with shrewd, appraising eyes. This was Speed's own entry, and though he half hoped Cal Bradley would win, the flimsy thing of wood and steel which bore the Kyle Aircraft Eagle carried all Speed's hope for immediate glory.

"Wish Bill had some of Cal's fire," he growled. "That ship of mine is twice as good as Cal's. One of these days, Georgia, I'm going to sign up young Bradley and make a star out of him."

"You mean you'd like to have him race for you?"

"Why not? He's the coming bet of the country today, and with him at my sticks, we'd lead the field. I build 'em best, he flies 'em best. Say!" Speed's frown went away under the light of sudden inspiration—"Why don't you persuade him?"

Georgia's glance was meant to be withering, but at that instant the ship flashed across the starting line and captured all of Speed's attention.

Five hundred feet up, Cal Bradley looked to the right and left to assure himself that the other two contestants were regularly spaced out behind him and shot the gun up into its last notch. The three-hundred-horsepower engine chattered and clanked and sent four hundred and forty feet of air behind it in the space of a single second. Three hundred miles an hour, and the air speed indicator was creeping even higher.

It was good to have a live motor in front of him, a sensitive stick in his fingers and a hurtling plane around him. Up ahead there were pylons to turn and wind currents to fight, but they were still ahead. Right now, Cal Bradley was perfectly content to sit in his cockpit and fly.

Directly to the rear, Smoke Gregory was hurling his Jupiter Aircraft ship into Cal's wake. Third in line came Bill Conklin, in the Kyle Eagle. Ahead of them the checkered pyramid which was Pylon One was looming.

Cal settled himself on the cushion his parachute made and prepared for the vertical which would soon be his lot. He spared the briefest glance to the rear to make certain of his airway and saw that Smoke Gregory, in the Jupiter ship, was gaining.

It was apparent that Jupiter Aircraft was out to win the day. Jupiter was like that. If their ship wasn't fast enough, the contestants had to beware severed control wires and graphite-filled crankcases.

Pylon One loomed to Cal's left, a great checkered tower marking the first lap of the course. Cal's engine was booming and his plane was traveling at a little over three hundred and ten. Gritting his teeth against the unconsciousness which would be his in an instant, he slapped his ship into a steep vertical and went around. He felt himself crushed against his parachute. Everything went black, as the centrifugal force dragged the blood away from his head. But it was always that way, and almost before he realized what he did, the plane was level once more and heading for Pylon Two at five miles a minute.

The fields below dissolved into a monotone of green. Only the clouds above were distinguishable. The motor, heating up, dropped a note in pitch.

Unconsciousness again, right side up again, and Cal was heading for Pylon Three and the field. Behind him, coming closer, was the Jupiter ship, with Gregory's black hood showing above the motor cowl. Cal's plane had skidded on a turn and was losing rapidly.

And then Cal Bradley heard his engine's mighty song drop another notch in tone. He cast worried eyes at the panel and saw that his oil was getting hot. He was losing speed, and behind him Gregory's cowl grew large.

The field was becoming more distinct. Cal could see the grandstand, with its rows of upturned faces and its fluttering pennants. He could see the ships on the line—the hundreds of them from every part of the country and globe. He could even see the oil trucks, where the refueling was done.

The roar of his engine was dimming rapidly and his eyes narrowed until only a slit of blue could be seen through his goggles. His hand on the stick was white.

A flash of color to the left caught Cal's attention. It was Gregory drawing abreast of him full gun. And while his glance still lingered, Cal saw that Gregory was about to cut diagonally across Cal's nose.

7

Cal tensed, knowing too well what his own immediate fate would be. If his plane was caught in the area of disturbed air behind the Jupiter ship, he would crash. It was not until then that Cal remembered Georgia's premonition, and remembered it too late.

He felt his stick loosen in his fingers. The nose of his plane went down. The ground grew twisty and brown through the arc of his propeller. Without having time to think, Cal yanked back on his stick and sent the racing ship hurtling straight up toward the sun. But no plane built so light could withstand the terrific pressure on its wings.

Eight hundred feet above the ground, spinning straight up, the plane shed its right wing in a shower of splinters.

Cal's fingers went to his belt and snapped the buckle open. His legs fought against the ship's motion. The ship turned and headed downward at a speed over two hundred miles an hour.

With something like a prayer, Cal Bradley flung himself away from his shattered plane and pulled the rip cord of his chute at the same instant. No time here to count to three—the ground was hazy with nearness, the brown gravel was a racing blur beneath.

Cal felt himself rolling over and over through space. Something slithered out behind him, and then he fell straight long enough to make a bet with himself whether or not the chute would stop him before the ground did.

A giant tug against his shoulders and legs told him that the silk above had filled, and he began to swing like the pendulum of some huge clock.

Sighing with relief, Cal took his opportunity to look around. Not until then did he see that his plane had crashed in the middle of the field. It was blazing cheerfully—fifteen thousand dollars' worth of racing ship, and all of Cal Bradley's hopes. The plane was to have brought him prize money by the hatful and contracts by the score—but there it lay, a burning shambles.

And then Cal saw something else. He was gently coming down near the microphones in front of the grandstand.

Holding himself limp, he felt the ground strike his feet. The chute turned him, and then pulled him over on his back while he fought to get at the shrouds. The wind was towing him along the ground and sending up a geyser of fine yellow dust.

Line by line, Cal gathered in his shrouds until he could touch the edge of the silken hemisphere and spill out the wind.

Hands began to strip the harness from him. Other hands relieved him of the chute. Testing himself gingerly the while, Cal stood up and looked for Georgia.

An announcer was pulling at him. "Come up and tell the crowd you're all right."

"Sure," said Cal, and went.

"Hello, folks," he said. "I'm all right."

A cheer roared down to him like the bursting of waves on a beach, and then Speed Kyle had him by the shoulder. "Good stuff, Cal. That was quick work."

Cal nodded. "I'd show you some quicker work if I could get my hands on Smoke Gregory. The son of a gun did that on purpose, Speed!"

9

"Sure he did," agreed Speed, quite cheerfully. "But that's no call to go brawling about it."

Georgia laid her hand on Cal's dusty jacket sleeve, her face white, her mouth trembling. "I don't like to say 'I told you so,' but—"

"Sure," said Cal, "go ahead, if it will make you feel any better. I'm sorry I scared you, honey, but I couldn't help it, honest."

Speed laughed. "Go on, couldn't you help it? Listen, Cal, I've something to ask you."

"Shoot."

"You haven't any plane now, and a pilot without a plane is as bad as a duck without wings. How about working for me?"

Cal looked at Georgia with mock menace. "Did you put him up to this?"

"No!" boomed Speed. "She's against my doing it. How about it?"

Out in the center of the field, the remains of Cal Bradley's plane crackled dismally. Cal frowned sadly in its direction, then nodded. "Okay, Speed. I'll push your jalopies around, so long as it isn't a family affair."

But before Speed Kyle could answer, a thundering roar burst out of the stands—laughter from ten thousand throats. It was not until then that Cal saw the microphone beside him and realized that every word he had spoken had been dinned through the surrounding countryside. The announcer grinned and ducked out of reach.

CHAPTER TWO

Loser's Pay

O VERHEAD, planes were circling, waiting for the landing flag, and the drone of their combined motors made speech difficult. The crowd was even larger on this second day of the meet, and from the air the ground had the appearance of a mammoth anthill, specked here and there by the idle wings of some great insect.

Bill Conklin, short and cheerful, was trying to match the lanky stride of Cal Bradley and failing.

"Don't think I'm sore," he said. "I've been praying for this to happen, Cal. Speed builds ships that are too damned fast, if you ask me. Why, man alive, it takes me two or three seconds to come to after I round a pylon in that racing job. One of these days I'm going to wake up and hear Gabriel blow assembly and find out that I smeared in. Not that it's worrying me, of course."

"There's enough work for two or three pilots, anyway," Cal said. "Test piloting and speed piloting are two different animals."

Bill grinned. "Maybe different, but they've both got horns. When I shed my wings I want space underneath, I'll tell a man! Well, there's Speed talking to Gregory. Who's the big fat bird with the cigar?"

11

"McNallan," said Cal, slowing down, "head of Jupiter Aircraft." He came to a full stop just within earshot of the group.

"That's all right, too," Speed was saying out of a tight mouth. "But we've got to keep this game clean, McNallan. This isn't the old auto racing game, not by a long shot. It used to be smart to fix the other fellow's motor, but it's not any more. And if you try any monkey business around my ships, you're going up before the NAA in a rush."

"Yah!" jeered McNallan, working furiously at his cigar. "Listen to who's talking! How about that time you put Hedley through the fence at Indianapolis? How about that, hey?"

"Hedley asked for it," said Speed, "and he got it. It was either him or me. Now this is different. I know the winner of the transport race will get the Amalgamated contracts for three hundred ships, and I know the altitude winner will reap the South American mail run bids. But that's nothing to kill a pilot over."

Cal swung lazily forward, his face a noncommittal mask. "What's up, Speed? These jaspers bothering you?"

"Oh, hello, Cal. I was just telling McNallan something for his own good."

"Yeah," said McNallan. "He means I was just telling him that if he intended to try for the Amalgamated and South American contracts, he'd have a dead pilot on his hands—maybe two."

"A fellow threatened me once," said Cal, still lazy.

"So what?" rasped Gregory.

"They buried him."

McNallan's face went redder. Gregory hefted a dangerous fist, and then thought better of it. Together they turned and walked into a hangar.

"You made 'em mad," said Speed.

"No!" snapped Bill.

"All right, wise guy," replied Speed, "I didn't see you winning any races yesterday."

Bill Conklin's expression froze on his usually cheerful face. He swallowed hard and started to move away, but Speed stopped him.

"Sorry," said Speed. "I didn't mean it that way, Bill. I'm just upset, that's all."

Cal lounged against the turtleback of a racing ship. "What's on the docket today, boss?"

"Boss!" snorted Speed. "Where do you get that stuff?"

"All right—Daddy, then," Cal grinned, and watched Speed's expression. "What am I supposed to fly?"

"That thing you're using for an armrest," growled Speed. "It's the KA 6, exhibition stunting. Do you want to do it, or shall we let Bill try his hand?"

"It's Cal's show," Bill said.

"Who told you I was a stunt pilot?" Cal said.

"Bird told me." And Speed turned to see Georgia getting out of her roadster.

She came toward them, her white sports dress shimmering like the surface of a pool.

"Hello, Cal!" she said. "Going upstairs?"

"Reckon so, honey. Speed tells me I've got to turn this thing wrong side in for the prize money."

She came closer, unsmiling. "Your chute all right? I'd die if—"

"Ssshhh!" cautioned Cal. "Let's see if there's any microphone around here first."

Georgia smiled, but the droning planes overhead drowned her sigh.

"Is the ship all right?" she asked Speed.

"Did you ever see a ship of mine that wasn't?" he said indignantly.

"I know," said Georgia. "But I heard some talk about McNallan."

"Where?" came from three throats at once.

Georgia looked around to be sure they were alone before she went on. "When you said that about Gregory on the microphone yesterday, Cal—"

"About Gregory crashing me on purpose?"

"Yes. Well, when you said that, the NAA started to investigate, and they almost threw Jupiter Aircraft out of the meet. McNallan boasted that he'd get you, Cal."

Speed raised his bushy white brows and rumbled deep in his throat. He turned and bellowed "Shorty!" into the hangar. When that mechanic came forth, he was ordered to go over the KA 6 with minute care.

Cal lounged around the ship and did some inspection on his own hook. "Is a Jupiter ship in this stunting contest?"

"Uh-huh," replied Speed. "Very much so. But don't worry, old son, you'll have all the air to yourself."

Georgia stood back and followed Cal with worried eyes.

14

Finally he went up to her and planted his feet wide apart, his arms akimbo.

"You haven't had any more hunches, have you?" he demanded.

Georgia averted her eyes and said nothing. Cal shrugged and walked away.

"Have you?" Speed asked her.

"Yes," she whispered.

But before her father could even whistle, a messenger ran up and handed Cal his orders to get on the line.

Cal climbed into the single-seater stunt plane and squirmed down until only the top of his head showed above the brilliant yellow fuselage. He gunned the engine experimentally, while Speed forgot his worries long enough to step back and admire this trim thing of compact beauty which was the handiwork of his aircraft factory.

Georgia came close to the cockpit and extended her hand, smiling. "Happy landings, Cal, and please don't try any more than the ship will stand."

Cal reached his gloved right hand over the side and clasped hers. He grinned, released his grip, waved to Bill and Speed and taxied off toward the starter's flag.

Georgia, in her abstraction, forgot to protect her face from the slipstream dust. She coughed now and dabbed at her eyes with a bit of lace and color. Then suddenly she shook her hand.

"Ouch!" she said.

"What's the matter?" said Speed.

"I guess . . . I must have burned my hand."

"Burned!" Bill Conklin took the hand gently and inspected

it. Suddenly he whipped out his handkerchief and scrubbed the girl's fingers with vigor.

"Get some soda!" He snapped, his eyes worried.

"*Soda!*" snorted Speed.

"Yes, soda! That's the stuff for acid burns. Where the devil could you have got that stuff on your fingers?"

Georgia would have passed her hand over her eyes, but Bill restrained her. Speed put his arm about her shoulders and hailed Shorty.

"Go for an ambulance!" he snapped. And then to Georgia, "What happened? You look like a ghost!"

"Cal!" gasped Georgia. "I got it off his glove, Dad . . . I must have! Why . . ." She winced and whipped at her hand again, as the acid began to bite home.

"Cal!" Bill snapped. "You mean you got that from Cal's glove? My lord Speed, Cal got it off his wires then!"

"You mean the wires of the KA 6 got acid on 'em?" Speed groaned as the truth went home. "Why, the dirty hounds—it's murder!"

Georgia looked at him whitely.

"He'll crash? Cal will crash?"

But Speed didn't have the heart to tell her the truth. Only he and Bill knew that the cables of the KA 6 had been impregnated with metal-eating acid, and that wires would part in the first maneuver Cal tried.

It was too late to stop Cal Bradley. Seconds ago he had hurled his stunting plane into the clear blue sky, prepared to turn it inside out in the stunt contest. . . .

"He'll crash? Cal will crash?"

Cal spiraled up, working his plane to an altitude of better than the fifteen-hundred-foot minimum the Department of Commerce set for stunting. He was all alone in the sky, now that all other planes had been called in, and he could look down upon the surrounding miles of checkerboard countryside and the hundreds of ships lined up near the hangars.

He was fourth in the line of contestants, and the three who had gone before had not, in Cal's estimation, done anything spectacular. They had held themselves down to standard stuff, counting upon precision to get them the money. Cal patted himself on the back, patted the KA 6, and told it that it had some violent surprises in store.

When he had reached two thousand feet, he snap rolled, to iron out the kinks, completely unaware of the rapidly weakening fine wires which held the wings in place. From the cockpit he could not see the brown splotch that was turning white on the cable under the left span.

He settled himself comfortably and snap rolled again in the reverse direction. He put down the nose and felt the plane lurch as it rocketed into its power dive. Slowly and with deftness he pulled back the stick and hurled the KA 6 into a perfectly circular loop, cutting the gun on top, to preserve its symmetry.

The KA 6 looped again, as smooth as oil, sending the shattering howl of its engine down against twenty thousand spectators in the stands.

Cal dived sharply and saw the speed indicator creep up. He pulled the stick, stepped on a rudder and went skyward like a corkscrew. And then he settled himself to the task of winning prize money.

At twenty-five hundred feet he turned the ship on its back, nose thrust down. Hanging there by his safety belt, he began to gun the engine and nurse his inverted rudders. Easily, gradually, as though it was nothing at all, instead of a highly sensational stunt, he dropped earthward in a perfect, inverted falling leaf.

At fifteen hundred feet he did an outside loop and came out of it, going back up again in a swoop which pressed him back with a heavy hand.

And then he started a series of tight loops, for there was no one there to tell him that the flying wires of his left wing were almost gone. He went over on his back the fourth time in a row. Then, unexpectedly, something hit him across the helmet and smashed the lens of his goggles.

Cal swore, shook the glass away from his face and tried to look up. An empty sensation in his stomach told him that he was spinning tightly.

Over his head he saw the wing section pinning him down into the cockpit. For a split second he regarded the great N painted there with wonder, and then he realized that his flying wires had broken and that the wing had folded back to trap him helpless in a ship spinning in from a height of two thousand feet.

Cal unbuckled his safety belt with a jerk so violent that he almost severed the web straps. He flung up his arms, trying to rid himself of the wing section—but the wind pressed the linen against the cockpit and was not so easily removed. Trying to stand, Cal tore at the wing with his gloved hands, noticing dully that the leather had been eaten away from his right fingers.

He saw his altimeter creeping down toward five hundred feet, and he leaped upward with tremendous force.

Motor screaming, wires shrieking, the crowd below hushed and on their feet, Cal burst through the obstruction and shot into space, hurled far away from the ship, which had almost been his coffin. His fingers fought to catch the rip cord of his parachute, but the metal was elusive.

Cal looked down full into the faces of the crowd and found himself hoping that his ship wouldn't crash into them.

And then he had the rip cord. The chute whipped away, jerking him harshly. After that he was swinging and floating through space, and listening to the echo of the sound his ship had made when it crashed. Something like a hurricane came up at him, and he knew it was the sigh of relief from the crowd. Hanging there over emptiness made Cal dizzy—it wasn't like having good, solid linen about him.

He slipped his chute until he could land in the parking space behind the stand, and he went so far as to pick out the car on which he expected to land. It was a mighty thing, that car, and its roof looked inviting. There were silver fixtures above its windshield which would offer good handholds.

His feet struck and his hands clenched, and he felt as if something was tearing him apart—it was just the wind in his chute. He held on, and then people were folding the silk and he was able to get up.

A man with an ugly, beet-red face was getting out of the car.

"Get the devil off there, you!" said the driver.

Obligingly Cal got off, and stood rubbing his shoulders where the harness had bit deep. People were laughing at the driver and calling to Cal.

Speed came up, limping and puffing.

"Sorry I lost your ship," Cal said.

"Ship!" snorted Speed. "Don't worry about ships, I got a factory full of 'em! I'm glad Georgia didn't see that, young man."

"I'm glad, too. Where is she?"

"She's in the hospital, with her hand all burned up with acid."

Cal blinked, his blue eyes growing light with worry. "How the—"

"You handed it to her," said Speed. "You wiped your hand over your flying wire and got it on your glove. And when she shook hands with you, she got it. Those damn Jupiter Air fiends!"

"Wait a minute!" said Cal. "You mean I had acid on my flying wires? How the devil did it get there?"

"McNallan or Gregory put it there when they were talking to me, the pups! It didn't burn through until you'd done a lot of stunts. That's why you crashed."

Cal set his lean jaw. "Is Georgia seriously hurt?"

"She's not feeling too good," snapped Speed. "I been looking for McNallan with one eye and waiting for you to crash with the other. I'm going to bend a monkey wrench over that bird's head!"

"Not until I've had *my* chance," said Cal. "You can deal

21

with what I leave. It's bad enough to crack me up, without hurting Georgia!"

And he hurried Speed Kyle away from there, without noticing that the red-faced gentleman of the car watched them with a sly sneer.

CHAPTER THREE

Undercover Men

IN the sheet-iron shack that served as the headquarters of Jupiter Aircraft, Smoke Gregory tried to hide his agitation by leaning his chair against the wall and putting his boots on the desk. McNallan glowered at the boot soles and shifted the cigar in his teeth.

"I can't help it if it didn't work. I told you Cal Bradley had nine lives." Gregory paused in his defense long enough to light a cigarette. "Besides, McNallan, you pay me to fly. That's my job, and if you want me to turn gangster, you'll have to raise the ante, and raise it plenty."

"Yah!" grated McNallan. "Haven't I pulled you up by the bootstraps and made a star out of you? And if you win this meet, you'll be famous. How about that? Besides, *Mister* Gregory, you're in this thing just as deep as I am."

"So what?" said Gregory.

"If you don't keep on playing ball, I'll spike your guns for you. We've got to get two contracts, pilot—but, then, you wouldn't be interested in the details. It's up to you to win this freak altitude stunt and the passenger plane race, too. If you don't, you'll have no more job than a rabbit."

"Neither will you," Gregory said drily.

McNallan spat in the general direction of the door. "You're getting smart, Gregory."

"Hell!" said the pilot. "That isn't news. Everybody on the field knows you'll go broke if you don't land the Amalgamated job and the mail contract."

"But I've got ideas—lots of ideas. Do you think this guy Conklin could win either event?"

Gregory blew out a blue smoke ring and nodded. "Speed events aren't his meat, but height events are."

"Then if we got Bradley out of the way, we'd still have Conklin on our hands. That right?"

"Probably. What you driving at?"

McNallan permitted himself a grin. "I've got an idea how we can get Bradley, and if there isn't any Conklin to take his place, Kyle will be up against it."

"Going to bump Cal Bradley on the ground?" asked Smoke coolly.

"No, we're not going to touch Bradley again—he's too lucky. But I've got ideas, Mister Gregory, that'd make your hair stand on end."

"Uh-huh. But count me out on any more rough stuff. I'm scared to death now, wondering if Speed Kyle will fix up one of my ships. Get yourself a flock of gangsters. Chi isn't so far away."

McNallan smiled again. "How do you know I haven't done that?"

"Guess some birds would do anything for a couple of million dollars," ventured Gregory, and he might have gone on if it had not been for a sudden apparition in the doorway.

McNallan followed his pilot's amazed glance and then saw

that he had visitors. Cal Bradley, his flying coat ripped, his hands scratched, stood a step in advance of Speed Kyle. Their expressions were far from peaceable.

"Thanks for the crash," said Cal, evenly. "It's great for publicity."

"Yeah," growled Speed. "How's your health, McNallan?"

McNallan snorted. "Why worry about my health?"

"Oh, I'd just hate to have you die while you were getting beaten up, that's all." Speed stepped out into the middle of the floor. "I told you we were going to tangle, McNallan, and I meant it."

"I suppose you went squealing to the NAA," said the head of Jupiter Aircraft.

Speed grunted. "No, we didn't go any place but right here. After we get through with you, you won't care anything about air meets, much less contracts. This is our fight, personal, and we intend to lick you every way for Sunday. Savvy?"

McNallan looked at the grim, lightly poised Cal, then glanced back to assure himself that Smoke Gregory hadn't run. His face took on an angry hue and his cigar jutted up at a forty-five degree angle.

"Just a couple of roughnecks," he said. "You'd better get out before I get sore."

And then the cigar spread out like an umbrella and McNallan lurched back against his desk, spluttering in rage and pain. Dazedly he regarded the bruise on Speed Kyle's knuckles.

Gregory heaved himself up and made a pass at Cal, but

25

*Cal Bradley, his flying coat ripped, his hands scratched,
stood a step in advance of Speed Kyle. Their
expressions were far from peaceable.*

the move was ill-timed and he sat back in his chair, his head rocking dizzily. In an instant, Cal reached out and brought the pilot standing, then sent him down again with a force which threatened the weak legs of the chair.

"Get up," said Cal distinctly. "You wouldn't let a little thing like that get you down, would you?"

Smoke Gregory shook the haze out of his eyes and tried to get up again. Then he looked sideways at McNallan and changed his mind. McNallan was poised on the edge of his desk, ready to slide off at the slightest jar. Speed Kyle furnished the motive power, and McNallan dropped, hitting the planks with a sodden thud.

"That being that," said Speed, "let me warn you that I don't tolerate any tinkering around my ships. And if you try it again, just remember what happened to Hedley at Indianapolis. We're not going to report you to the NAA, because there's no satisfaction in that. We're going to beat you at your own game, savvy?"

McNallan, staring up with half an eye, was too far gone to nod. He could only sigh with relief when he saw his visitors depart. When he was quite sure that they had gone, he raised himself up on a dusty elbow and looked at Gregory.

"I've got an idea, Gregory," he said thickly.

"Keep it!" snapped his pilot, fingering his damaged face.

"Yeah, but this hasn't anything to do with rough stuff. That Speed Kyle is going to regret the day he was ever born."

Outside, walking back to their headquarters, Speed Kyle forgot his limp and even went so far as to strut.

"That'll teach 'em," he said. "And if they try any more funny business, we'll do it again."

Cal looked ahead and said nothing. He was watching for a swirl of silk and his mind was not quite at ease concerning the late demonstration.

"Georgia ought to be around by this time," said Speed, sensing Cal's thoughts. "I don't think she was hurt much."

"I hope not."

"I'm out to get those contracts for a lot of reasons," Speed continued. "You and Georgia, for two."

"Why us?"

"Well, it's kind of nice to have a business that'll buy your groceries at least."

"It isn't that bad, is it?" Cal said. "I thought you had a factory full of ships."

Speed's eyes lost some of their sparkle and he started to limp again, as though the question had caused all his years to descend upon him.

"That's it, Cal. I've got a factory full of ships, and no market for 'em. I've got eighteen transport planes of the kind Amalgamated Airlines wants. Have you any idea how much they cost to build?"

"Ten thousand dollars."

Speed grunted. "Ten thousand, and then some. Eighteen ships at ten thousand dollars apiece is a hundred and eighty thousand dollars. I've got that tied up in transport planes alone. And then there's these fast, mail-carrying altitude ships I thought I could sell to the Andes Mail. That's another hundred thousand."

"What did you build them for?" Cal demanded.

"They promised to buy 'em, that's why. But they didn't put it down in writing, and when they heard that the National Air Meet was featuring some fast climbing and altitude tests, they decided to wait. Jupiter Aircraft is the only one that builds a ship like mine—not nearly as good, but cheap. And Jupiter Aircraft is angling for the Amalgamated contracts, just as I am. And they only built *one* ship to do it."

"So it's kind of crucial," said Cal.

"You bet it is! I've got ideas about your future, Cal. I always wanted you to fly for me, and now I want you as a technical advisor and general manager. I'm getting old, Cal, and if you were to marry Georgia and settle down to running the plant, I'd be tickled silly. But if I don't get any contracts—well, there won't be any plant. Savvy?"

"Yes. And I'm more than—look, there's Georgia now."

Georgia, carrying her right hand in a sling made of parachute silk, climbed down from her car and stood waiting for them. Her eyes were calm, but her mouth showed suffering and strain. She didn't speak until Cal stopped beside her and leaned against the radiator.

"You're not hurt, are you, Cal?" she asked, her voice even.

"Who, me?" Cal grinned. "You couldn't hurt me with an ax."

"Don't be smart just to keep me from worrying, Cal."

Cal stopped grinning. "How's the hand, honey? That was a dirty trick I played on you, wasn't it?"

"It wasn't your fault," said Georgia, moving closer. "It's all right now. Just a little burn.

"Cal . . ." she paused and looked at Speed with eyes deep and black and baffling.

Speed yawned elaborately and moved away. "Be seeing you, kids. There's work to be done."

They watched him go and then Georgia laid her slim white fingers on Cal's tattered sleeve. Gravely he waited for her to speak.

"Listen, Cal, I—" She stopped, averting her eyes. "They say accidents go in threes. You know that, don't you?"

"Sometimes they do—but not when somebody else is causing them. That's different."

"Not different, Cal. I . . . I don't think I can stand it."

All compassion, he stood up straight and laid an arm about her shoulder. "Can't stand what?"

"Your crashing again. Honest, Cal, I don't mean to be a wet blanket, though I know it seems that way. But can't you, for my sake, stay on the ground the rest of the meet? There isn't anything more important than you."

He looked in the direction Speed Kyle had taken, sudden knowledge making his eyes dark, as he realized that Speed Kyle had not told Georgia of his financial straits. Otherwise, Georgia would never have asked this favor—or would she have asked it anyway?

"I can't do that, Georgia. Your dad's bought my services, and I can't let him down. He needs me right now, as he's never—I mean, it wouldn't be fair to him."

Georgia looked away, her dark eyes brooding on space. When she looked back at Cal, her face showed strain. She put her hand on his arm, and said in earnest pleading:

"Then, if you can't promise that, Cal, tell me you won't do any more stunting and that you'll stay out of high-speed races. Will you?"

Cal thought rapidly. The altitude test was not stunting, and the transport race was not high speed. The least he could do would be to place her mind at rest.

"All right," he said. "I promise not to do any more stunts, and not to enter any high-speed events. Is that better?"

Georgia's smile said that it was.

CHAPTER FOUR

Cloud-Bound

BILL CONKLIN sang off key about a dying aviator who pleaded to have various parts of his ship removed from his anatomy, but Bill was quite cheerful. He sat upon an engine crate and wiped a piece of rubber with a straggly tuft of cotton waste. The mask in his hands was attached to a small liquid oxygen tank of polished metal—the equipment of an altitude flyer.

Cal Bradley stood for a moment in the door before he entered.

"Cheerful, aren't you," remarked Cal.

"Hello," said Bill. "Some crowd out today, isn't there? Always better the third day, anyway."

"Speed tells me you're taking the KA 80 on a cloud jaunt today."

"Sure," Bill grinned. "Think I'd polish up a mask for you? That's my meat—altitude. Kind of surprised me, though. I thought you had it on your docket. Speed must have changed his mind."

Cal didn't say that he thought somebody had changed Speed's mind for him. He merely picked up the cylinder and looked it over.

"Valves seem okay," he said. "Be the devil if dirt got into them, huh?"

"Sure would," Bill agreed. "But I cleaned it all out. When do I start?"

Cal looked at his watch and frowned. "Fifteen minutes, Bill. Guess I'll go out and get that ship to ticking over for you." And he stepped out of the hangar and walked to the side of the mail plane which would, with luck, be flying over the Andes in a few months.

Bill put on the chamois mask, looking like some medicine man out of Africa. His air bubbled through the mouthpiece and whistled through the vaporizing coils. Satisfied, Bill took it off and gave it a final rub, spitting to rid his mouth of the rubber taste.

He was about to get up when a door creaked at the back of the hangar and he glanced back to see a thick-set man with a beet-red face entering, followed closely by another dressed in flashy clothes.

"Hello, pilot," said the red-faced individual. "Going to take an altitude hop?"

"Uh-huh," Bill grunted.

"Then you're Bradley. That right?"

"No, Cal Bradley's out starting the ship."

"Oh, I see. Then you're Conklin."

Bill stood up and turned toward the door, handling the oxygen mask with care.

"Wait a minute," said the red face. "I've got something to say to you."

But Bill Conklin didn't turn. He was too used to curious bystanders about the hangars to pay any more attention.

Besides, he had only a few minutes to get his ship on the line. But suddenly he heard a footstep and whirled.

Above him, blue and ugly, a gun butt was coming down at his head. He saw it and tried to throw up his arms, dodging as he did so, but the gun was quicker, and the whack it made against the pilot's skull was drowned in the thundering roar of the ship outside.

The red-faced intruder eased the short, chunky Conklin to the floor. "Pick him up, Tony, and carry him out to the car."

"Gosh!" Tony grunted, his thin face twitching. "You croaked him."

The red-faced man grinned wryly.

"What if I did?"

Tony winced.

"They didn't say to croak him. They just said to put some sand into that thing there."

The red-faced one reached down and retrieved the oxygen mask. Unscrewing the mouthpiece, he let a handful of dust pour into the tubes. Then, carefully wiping away all signs of handling, he laid it down on the motor crate.

Tony, dragging at the pilot's armpits, backed toward the rear door. "They didn't say to do it this way, pal, but I guess it's all right."

"Sure it's all right. I'd hate to be the guy that puts that thing on and tries to breath through it."

He opened the back door and helped his partner at the task of placing the inert Bill Conklin into the back of a huge silver-appointed sedan.

Speed Kyle looked over the mail ship for the tenth time and then came back to Cal, glancing at a gigantic nickel-plated watch.

"What's holding Bill?" Speed growled. "He's got two minutes to get started. Rout him out, Cal."

Cal nodded and ambled into the hangar, coming back presently with the oxygen mask and container.

"No sign of him," he said. "Wonder what's happened."

"Might have been taken sick," ventured Speed, frowning so that his bushy white brows almost covered his eyes. "Was he all right when you saw him?"

"Right as rain. If he doesn't show up in the next thirty seconds, I'll have to take her up."

"No, no," said Speed, hurriedly.

"Why not?"

Speed took a sudden interest in the starter out in the center of the field.

"I said, why not?" Cal repeated. "Georgia isn't around to catch you up on it."

"How'd you know she made me—" Speed stopped, grinning like a small boy caught in the jam pot.

"Look the other way, Speed. And when you find something so interesting that you can't take your eyes off it, you'll hear the KA 80 start out to break the altitude record."

Accordingly, Speed found the hangar side to be of interest, and, obeying orders, he didn't look up until Cal had settled into the pit, or until the mail plane was halfway to the line. Then he waved, and Cal, sitting over his stick, waved back.

The mail plane, capable of carrying a ton payload, stopped on the line in front of the grandstand, motor idling. Cal sat still and regarded his instrument panel, waiting for his orders and his sealed altimeter.

A sweating, florid gentleman handed him a wooden box which held the official barograph and muttered something about luck before he turned away.

The voice in the loudspeakers was bellowing as it always did, and the crowd was staring at the squat, sleek ship which bore the Kyle Aircraft Eagle.

"Out there," said the announcer, like a circus ballyhoo artist, "you see Cal Bradley in the KA 80 mail plane. Cal's the boy you saw float to safety two days in succession when his planes went into their death dives. Now he is about to try for the altitude record for his class of ship. He is carrying a dummy cargo of mail weighing one thousand pounds. Okay, Cal—good luck!"

The starter waved a green-checkered flag and Cal poured on the coal. Five hundred horses shot him down the field like a green javelin and hauled him into the air. That done, he sat back and took a deep breath, accustoming himself to the feel of the controls and the snarl of his huge engine. He did a gradual climbing turn, then put the nose just under its point of stall and went roaring skyward into the occasional cumulus overhead.

The oxygen mask hung about his neck, swaying as the ship hit air bumps, but the motor's drone was too loud to permit Cal to hear the rasp of sand shifting within the mouthpiece.

When he got up to the twenty-five-thousand-foot level he'd put it on—but not till then. When his heart began to hammer and his lungs began to throb for lack of air, and when his arms became too heavy and when his judgment went bad, he'd use the tank—but not before. To date, no man had put a thousand pounds of mail above all records, and Cal intended to be the first. He had the ship, and he had the day.

The altimeter went to ten thousand feet almost before Cal had settled himself securely in the pit. The five hundred horses were going strong, and the whine of the supercharger sounded like the battle scream of a prehistoric dragon. He did an easy turn, placing himself over the diminutive field below, and caused the white needle to creep up five thousand.

From fifteen thousand feet, roads were strings, planes were bright dots against the ground and the hangars were cardboard toys carved by delicate hands. The fields were small rectangles totally lacking in detail. People, aside from the dark blot in the stands, were too small to be distinguished.

Cal watched the horizons stretching out and lost in haze, and wondered how far a man would have to go to see the Earth as a ball. He was at eighteen thousand feet, and even here he could see the distinct curvature of the surface. The world was no longer a tabletop.

He glanced at the wooden box and the face of the sealed barometer, wondering how long it would take for the judges to send it to Washington for accurate reading. It might be two or three days, maybe more, before he'd know whether or not he had broken the record.

Tentatively, he removed his goggles and placed the chamois

mask over his face, not yet placing the mouthpiece and nose clamp in position.

Five hundred horses snorted in unison, the supercharger fed its air with a siren blare, and the air was thin. Cal's heart was beating a steady but fast tattoo against his ribs, and his lungs began to burn. However, he needed air higher up. Not yet would he drain on the tank.

The altimeter needle hovered over the mark which indicated twenty thousand feet, but when he looked at it, Cal was unable to fix his mind on the figure. His arms were terribly heavy when he began to insert the mouthpiece and clamp the metal on his nose. Preparing to take a deep breath, he coughed suddenly and set his strained lungs throbbing. Certain that he had been mistaken, he breathed cautiously through the tank and again he coughed.

And then the knowledge that the oxygen tank was unfit came over him and he tore away the mask. Unscrewing the airtight mouthpiece, he inverted it and saw sand pour back into his slipstream.

His first impulse was to kick the ship into a spin and regain breathable air as quickly as possible, but he fought it down. This was the one chance allowed, and if he missed out this time, Kyle would sell no mail planes to the Andes outfit. Somewhere down in the grandstand some fellows with olive skin and correct clothes were looking up, trying to decide where they would invest a good many hundred thousand dollars.

Cal pulled back easily on the stick and fought off the darkness and went on up into a sky which was heightless and dark and cold. His heart was hammering like a pushrod, his breath, if he could have heard it, was rasping. His mouth was open and he could not close it, even though the whipping propeller blast robbed him of what little air there was left.

His right hand was locked around the stick, his left hand gripped hard at the throttle. Long ago he had taken his feet off the rudder bars. It was only necessary to go up, and then up again. Now and then the engine changed in tone, and when this happened, he brought every faculty to bear and forced the ship back into an even climb.

And then at last his hand was no longer able to stay on the stick. He could not see the altimeter, and he found strangely that he didn't care. Something told him to keep on going, but something else argued that it wasn't worth the price. He was aware of nothing but the cockpit around him. Mechanically his left hand went down to the stabilizer and he tugged it back. He didn't know that he was forcing the plane to keep on climbing without a guiding hand. Something in his skill as a pilot told him that. The stabilizer locked in climbing position, and then Cal suddenly discovered that he was talking with Georgia in a beautiful garden where a fountain roared like an airplane motor.

In the stands and on the field, those who had good eyes still saw the speck against the blue when the sun flashed off a silvered wing. Speed Kyle saw it and held his breath for a minute at a time, taking another only when his lungs protested. And then somebody was tugging at Speed's arm, and Georgia was there.

40

"Bill's certainly hitting the ceiling, isn't he?" she said.

"Bill!" said Speed, before he remembered. "Oh, yes, Bill."

Suddenly suspicious, Georgia cried, "Who is it?"

"Bill," Speed snorted. "Bill, of course."

"You can't lie to me, Dad—that's Cal! I can see it in your face that it's Cal. Oh, *why* did you let him go up?" There was no criticism in the voice, only fear, and the feeling that crashes always run in threes.

Speed put his arm around her, still looking up at the occasional flash of silver, and then he stiffened and his hand trembled on the girl's sling. The sigh of the crowd told Georgia that something was wrong. She looked up again, her expression unchanging. Her face went dead white.

The speck of silver was growing large. Twenty-odd thousand feet below it, they could see that something was wrong. The flash came regularly, like the ticking of a clock.

"He's spinning," said Speed in a matter-of-fact voice. "He's trying to get down as quick as he can."

Georgia tried to speak, but found that something had lodged in her throat. She wanted to tell Speed that Cal wasn't spinning because he wanted to spin. Her sixth sense—that thing given to all women whose men follow the trails of danger—told her that Cal was slumped unconscious in his pit, and that five hundred snarling horses and the tug of gravity were bringing him closer to destruction by the second.

The KA 80 grew in size until the wings were distinguishable, and then at fifteen thousand feet it started into a lunging, swooping dive that informed the crowd the ship was out of control. It spun for an instant, then started in a long plunge

41

which brought it to ten thousand feet. Motor full on, it was headed straight for the ground.

After that, the stricken ship went into a series of unfinished arcs. The howl of the racing motor hung like a pall over the stands. The pitch was changing like the cry of a wounded animal.

On its back, it plunged again, swooped out of it and came down until Speed could see Cal's head, lolling over the side of the pit. For an instant it righted itself and began to climb. It thrust up its blurry nose, then whipped down with the speed of light. Two thousand feet still remained between the plane and the ground.

Georgia watched it go into a plunge which seemed to be the end. And then she stumbled back against Speed and her eyes went shut and her mouth fell partly open. Scarcely noticing, Speed Kyle held her up, his own heart beating in his throat.

Cal Bradley's first intimation of his plunge was a swoop which banged his head into the crash pad before him. For a full ten seconds he looked at his instruments, uncomprehending, and then he caught sight of color a thousand feet underneath and knew that he was spinning down in a runaway ship.

His hands, shaky and unbelievably weak, fought for the lashing stick, but even when he neutralized the controls, nothing happened. Not until then did he understand that the act of fixing the stabilizer in an angle of climb had saved his life. Otherwise he would have gone in full gun.

He released the savior lever and pulled the plane out of

a spin. When he flew level once more, he saw the ground racing by a hundred feet below.

Ahead the grandstand loomed up. Cal hurdled it. He banked steeply and roared past the pennants once more. And then something prompted him to salute the crowd.

He saw them standing, and he saw their open mouths and knew that they were cheering. That was enough. Cal Bradley grinned and angled around to set his ship down upon the earth he had been so perilously close to leaving.

When his plane stopped floating, he set it down smartly and ground looped to go back in the direction of the lines. His hands were no longer shaking, for he had enough oxygen in his blood by now, but his brows knotted as he looked at the wooden box which held the official altimeter. It would be a long time before he found out whether or not the risk had been in vain.

And then he gunned the wheels over the line and stood up, to hear the bellowing loudspeakers and to see Georgia coming toward him.

Completely forgetting that she might have cause to call him down, only remembering that he had just pulled his life out of the fire, Cal jumped to the ground and went toward her.

"Cal," said Georgia, without any trace of emotion, "I only wanted to tell you that it's over."

"You bet it is," said Cal, not understanding. And then he saw the accusing light in her eyes.

"I mean you and me, Cal. I can't stand it, and you promised me yesterday not to do anything dangerous again during the meet. That wasn't so much to ask, was it?"

"But . . . but this wasn't high speed or stunting!"

"It was close enough," said Georgia. "When you think you can keep your promises to me, you can come back. Not until." And with that she walked toward her roadster.

"Well, I'll be—" Cal began.

Speed shrugged. "I can't figure 'em out either, old son. Her mother was just like that at times. She's just sore because she was weak enough to faint, that's all. She'll get over it."

But Cal Bradley wasn't convinced, and he pushed his way through the crowd toward a place where he could be alone and could soliloquize on the curious ways of women.

CHAPTER FIVE

Missing

"I guess," said Smoke Gregory, "that a fellow would do anything if he was offered a tall enough slice of cold, hard cash."

McNallan regarded his chief pilot across the scarred desk and chewed violently at his cigar. "You said that before, Gregory, and I won't deny it. And if I can get the business that way, I will. We used to do a lot worse in the old auto racing game."

"Yeah?" said Gregory. "The little plan you just outlined so calmly seems the height of something or other. As for me, I'm damned glad I never had to push racers on a board track, if that's the way you did it."

"But you haven't anything to squawk about here, have you? You turning tender-hearted all of a sudden?"

"No," said Gregory hesitantly. "The job's all right. But when it comes down to coldblooded murder—well, I tell you, I don't like it."

"It won't be murder, it'll just be a little accident. If that Cal Bradley has any brains at all, he'll sleep in his plane tonight, and that's all we need."

"But it won't seem logical if he's to run away right now, will it?"

McNallan chuckled. "It'll be plenty logical when I plant the stuff in his baggage. It's worth ten thousand dollars to me any day to cover us up. And don't worry about the gravy, Gregory—there's plenty of it. I've got it figured out how I can build the transport planes for Amalgamated for half the right price and sell them for half again as much."

"Hope you didn't gyp on the crate I've got to fly tomorrow."

"Hell, no!" snapped McNallan. "That ship's as good as gold. I'm talking about the standard production ones. Amalgamated will think this plane is a sample, and they'll bite."

"But they'll test them out, won't they?"

"Sure they will. We'll build 'em just strong enough to stand the test and a few flights. We'll deliver the works at the same time, and when they're paid for we'll close out our business. Reputation doesn't mean a thing, compared to the mazuma. I've got discarded engine parts by the carload. Bought them at a scrap sale. I can build the engines of those and go shy on the Duralumin in the wings, and we'll be sitting pretty."

"And if we get the Andes mail contracts?"

"Same thing. They won't know the difference. And I'm not worrying about how many pilots crack up in South America." McNallan sat back, smiling and regarding his cigar.

"Well," said Smoke Gregory, "I don't care what you build so long as I don't have to fly 'em, and so long as I get my cut. What time will we get Cal Bradley?"

"Make it ten. You can wander around until that time, but be sure you're back, and make certain that that chute is in good working order."

"You leave that part to me," said Gregory and stepped out on the almost-deserted airport. "There's a light in the Kyle hangar, so I guess your hunch was a good one."

The single yellow bulb did its best to drive away the shadows from the hangar corners. It shone upon the trim red bulk of a twin-motored, high-speed passenger plane and upon the hunched backs of Cal Bradley and Speed Kyle.

Speed, chin in hand, seated upon a stray parachute, idly kept his eye on the ship. "I guess you're right, Cal. Bill couldn't have just evaporated. Hope nothing very serious has happened to him."

Cal glanced out of the corner of his eye and then resumed his aimless task of stirring a piece of greasy cotton waste with a spare pushrod. He was seated on the wheel of the transport ship, his face in shadow.

"I don't think they'd pull anything as rough as killing a man outright," he said, trying to believe his words. "Maybe after the meet, Bill will turn up safe and sound. You know, I've always kind of liked that little cuss."

"Well, when I've got time to spare, I'm going to do some tall sleuthing." Speed emphasized it by kicking an oil drain can. "We've got nothing that'll hang Jupiter Aircraft. That is, we haven't yet. But when I get to working at a thing, I don't often let go. There'll be some kind of evidence—you wait and see. I got Evarts put behind bars for manslaughter once. He sent three birds through the fence all at one crack, and did it on purpose."

47

Cal nodded absently. He was busy with his own speculations.

"One thing sure," continued Speed. "Nothing'll happen to this baby tonight, with you sleeping here. I don't envy you the hard bed, though."

"I'll put cushions in the aisle," said Cal. "I've done it before. Back in the old barnstorming days I used to sleep in an open cockpit in cornfields and wake up soaked with dew."

"I always slept with my bus just before the Indianapolis. You've no idea how ornery human beings can be."

"McNallan's a fair example." Cal's voice was bitter.

They sat silent for long minutes. Then a light, vibrant voice from the doorway brought them both to their feet.

"Hello, owl," said Georgia. "You and I had better be getting to the hotel, Dad. It's past nine-thirty. I've been sitting out there in the car for hours."

Cal stepped forward, smiling, but then the yellow light fell on Georgia's face and Cal understood that the greeting and lightness were not for him, and stopped.

Speed Kyle limped out onto the tarmac and regarded the stars overhead. "Be a fine day for the race tomorrow, won't it, Cal?"

"Sure," agreed the pilot, looking at Georgia. But the girl turned her back and went out to her roadster, holding the door open for her father.

Before Speed climbed in, he shouted back to the lank shadow against the yellow bulb, "Get all the sleep you can. We've *got* to win in the morning!"

Cal waved and watched the ellipse the headlights made

against the concrete. He heard the gears clash, and then only the red border lights of the field were there to keep him company in his long vigil.

Cal was tired when he went back to the plane, tired mentally and physically. His head ached from the rapid change of altitude he had experienced that afternoon, and his ears felt as though they encased constantly burning metal stoppers. He shook his head as though to rid it of its misery, and then climbed up into the passenger cabin of the ship.

The aisle was several feet in length, and though it was closely bound on either side by wicker chairs, there was still room enough for a man to lie at length. Cal collected several leather cushions and threw them on the narrow carpet, preparing a bed which would be both chill and not too soft.

Speed had at first insisted that the vigil was his own right. Then he had dictated that a mechanic would stand the watch. But Cal remembered acid on his flying wires and sand in his oxygen tank and insisted on keeping watch himself. After all, it was his own life that was at stake.

Before he lay down upon the leather bed, he stepped forward and touched the control wheel he would fight on the morrow. In the shadowy light the instruments glowed like a stationary squadron of fireflies, and the polished mahogany shimmered dully.

In the accustomed confines of a plane cabin, looking down at familiar things, Cal felt some of the weariness and worry ease up. He had no particular fears about the coming day, for he was certain that the KA eight-passenger monoplane was a better ship than any Jupiter had ever manufactured.

He touched the twin throttles which controlled the two enormous engines and smiled. After that he felt better. He unlaced his boots and tied the strings around his ankles to give his legs a rest, then he laid himself down upon the improvised bed to make a bid for sleep.

Although the problem of Bill Conklin's mysterious disappearance hovered over his mind, he found himself slipping off into slumber, and told himself that he would wake at the slightest sound.

Unheeded, the luminous dial of his wristwatch ticked on methodically. The small second hand went around, matching the regularity of its owner's breathing, and then the two long streaks of phosphorus indicated that the hour was ten.

The hinges on the hangar door creaked softly, barely penetrating the gloom with their dismal sound. A cautious foot clanked against an oil drum. Cal Bradley stirred uneasily, weariness again pressing him into the depths of slumber. A hand reached through the yellow arc of light and silently pulled open the fuselage door.

The snick of metal cut into the quiet and gave Cal the first intimation of danger. He sat up straight, blinking, trying to tighten his muscles. And then the door on the other side of the cabin came open and a bulky shape catapulted in. Cal threw up his hands and caught at that body, immediately aware of another looming over a seat back above him.

"Give it to him!" snapped a voice.

A pistol butt came down, blurred and blue, but Cal shifted his head and caught the impact against his shoulder. His hands fought to imprison the body he had first grasped.

A wicker chair crashed down and blocked the aisle. The copilot's seat was knocked from its moorings, and the lurching figure Cal sought to hold crashed against the auxiliary controls and made the ailerons creak far out on the wings. The great ship seemed to quiver throughout its entire length.

A blue pistol butt still hovered in the air, the face behind it taut and watchful.

"Give it to him!" said a voice outside, and the man behind the weapon obeyed. Cal felt something explode against his skull and his hands felt queerly weak. His knees buckled slowly, and then, as though a string which held him up had been slashed, he sagged back upon the trampled leather cushions, inert and helpless.

"Okay, Gregory. We got him."

Smoke Gregory moved into the light and climbed up into the cabin. He stopped an instant and surveyed the fallen pilot. "Huh! He's still breathing!" He glanced about him, then set the copilot's seat back in place and pointed at it. "Lash him into that with some safety wire while I get into my chute."

"Okay." The man with the beet-red face lost little time in executing the command. He propped Cal up in the chair and lashed his hands behind him with the thin brass wire. Then he started on the ankles and suddenly discovered that he had run out of material.

"Snap into it!" said Gregory, wriggling into parachute harness.

The red-faced man shrugged and made Cal's shoelaces take the place of the wire. Wrapping the long laces around both ankles, he drew them tight to the chair legs and tied them with a hard knot. That done, he backed out of the cabin and made his way over to the hangar doors, which he rolled back.

"All set now?" he said to Gregory.

"Yeah. Scram." Gregory settled himself into the pilot's seat and reached down for the starters. He leaned sideways to assure himself that he had sufficient clearance on either side of the ship, and then adjusted the throttles. The twin engines below the wing began to churn, and the swinging props threw back the yellow light in a blurred arc.

With a snorting cough, the motors came alive. Gregory let off the brakes and let the big ship roll out to the tarmac. Allowing himself a little time for the warming of his power plants, Gregory coasted slowly toward the dark, deserted line. A watchman swung out of the operations office, blinking his flashlight.

"It's okay," Gregory shouted above the purring engines. "I'm Bradley, of Kyle Aircraft."

Apparently satisfied, the watchman went back to make a note in his log.

The big ship's tail came off and blasted down the runway, taking the air with a leap. The red boundary lights shot by below and the wind vane glow diminished rapidly behind them. All that remained of the mammoth port was the flashing red and white beacon on its far edge.

Evidently Gregory knew where he was going. Without swinging for altitude, he darted south at a hundred and eighty-five miles an hour.

Cal's head was jolted from side to side by the bumpy air, and Gregory glanced at him occasionally, his face thin and tight in the panel glow. Gregory glanced over the side every few seconds, then back at the board. He waited until the altimeter rested at two thousand feet before he leveled off.

And then Cal Bradley's voice fell smoothly on the pilot's ear.

"You don't," said Cal, "happen to have a cigarette, do you?"

Gregory jumped, then glared at the man in the copilot's seat. "You'll have enough fire *without* smoking, where you're going." He glanced uneasily over the side again. "You won't be so cocky in a couple of minutes."

Cal smiled slowly. "The same old Gregory. Mind telling me what's going to happen?"

"You'll find out soon enough."

"Don't expect to get away with this, do you?"

Gregory snorted. "Why not? Tomorrow they're going to find you burned up in this ship, and they're going to discover ten thousand dollars and a note from McNallan in your grips."

"Framed, eh?"

"Framed."

"And," said Cal, slowly, "how many people do you expect to believe that cock-and-bull story?"

"When they find out you threw Conklin into the river

because he found you out, they'll believe anything else we care to tell. How do you like them apples?"

"So Bill Conklin's dead, is he?"

"Sure he is. When they smashed his skull they had to get rid of him, didn't they?"

Cal's eyes glinted in the panel light and he moved his lashed hands restlessly. "Have they found his body yet?"

Gregory shrugged and looked over the side again, nodding with sudden satisfaction. "You'd better keep your date," he growled.

Slowly, Cal leaned sideways and looked down on his own side. In the center of an emergency landing field, close enough to the flashing beacon to be within its reflected sweep, a car's lights were visible, and even from two thousand feet it was possible to see the glinting silver above its windshield.

Gregory let the transport plane streak away from the field, preparatory to coming back.

"I'll be leaving you now," he said.

"Fine."

"*Not* so fine—as you'll find out in about two minutes." And Gregory reached down and adjusted the stabilizer until the ship stayed in a very gradual dive. "In a few minutes, you'll see the ground come up and meet you. The motors are both going strong, so you'll burn and nobody'll be the wiser." He glanced behind the copilot seat and saw the glint of a metal disk. "They'll know it's you all right when they read your identification plate. Tomorrow the papers will know all about how you bumped your friend Conklin, stole a ship and tried to lam."

Gregory banked the plane and started back toward the field, watching the beacon through the window. Cal regarded him narrowly, his mouth set and thin.

"Here's where I leave you," said Gregory. "And let me tell you this: if, by any chance, you happen to get out of this mess and get back to start that race tomorrow, you'll wish you'd ridden this crate in. We'll be watching the port, and if you come back, you won't have to worry about your girlfriend any more."

Cal watched the other open the door and slide out into the whipping propeller blast. He saw Gregory's hand go to the rip cord of the chute, and he saw empty space where Gregory had been an instant before. Below, outlined against the glow of the beacon and the headlights, the silken hemisphere of the chute blossomed in the darkness.

Cal glanced over at the altimeter and saw that he had nineteen hundred feet to go. The plane was flying itself, stabilizer set to hold it in the dive. It would go on for many miles before it finally crashed. With the ignition on, fire was certain.

Cal looked down at his feet and saw that they were strapped solidly to the legs of the squat leather chair, and while they were tied only with shoe strings, the number of turns made it impossible for Cal to break them. His hands were already sore and raw from twisting.

At fifteen hundred, the air bumps began to increase and Cal gave the bank and turn indicator a narrow scrutiny, wondering whether or not the wing would dip up far enough to send him into a spin. At each new lurch the seat shifted a little.

And then Cal deliberately began to sway himself off balance. With every bump, he exaggerated the tilt of his seat and found that the violent smash his assailant had given it had loosened its moorings.

He permitted himself no time to dwell upon his fate, and he tried hard to keep his faith in his luck. He winced when he remembered the threat to Georgia, but told himself he would have to take things as they came—one at a time. With the transport plane gone, and with no pilot to take his place, Speed Kyle would lose out all the way around. Even if he had beaten the altitude record, or even done as well as the Jupiter plane, the resulting business would hardly keep Kyle Aircraft going. A hundred and eighty thousand dollars is a lot of money to sink into transport planes.

And then came a bump larger than the others. Cal threw himself back, and felt the seat topple. He held his head on his chest to protect it from the crash of the fall to the cabin floor.

For an instant he saw lights bursting before his eyes and knew that he had succeeded in his plan. He lay inert, gathering his strength. His legs shot out with a sudden jerk and his bonds slipped off the chair legs, the laces hanging in great, tangled loops. That done, Cal hooked his right toe into his left heel and shed the boot. He repeated the operation and knew that his legs, at least, were free.

Squirming around, he pressed his soles against the panel and shoved up. Slowly his arms, which had been locked around the chair back, slid out and he found that he could climb to his knees.

He crouched in the narrow aisle, bracing himself against the repeated shock of bumps, and worked at his hands. The safety wire had been placed there after his arms had been wrapped around the chair back, and now, with that pressure gone, his hands slipped gradually out of the embrace of the loops. His left hand came first, and then, from where he knelt, he saw the dark silhouette of a tree loom beside the plane. That meant he was almost down on the ground.

With a quick lunge, he snatched at the control wheel and pulled back. Ahead he saw a hedge pass under him. A barn stood just beyond, and Cal pulled back and prayed that he would clear.

The plane almost scraped its wheels on the shingles as it passed over the obstruction, and then it was up and flying free. Suddenly weak, Cal slipped into the pilot's seat and reached for the rudders with his bootless toes, amazed at his success, and wondering if he were actually still alive or whether this was just a hazy dream. But the beacon to the south was real, and the stars that sparkled overhead were fixed and spinning like the inside of a cleaned gun barrel. To the north a lighted haze showed the city's position. Cal banked slowly around and headed for it.

For several reasons he did not take the opportunity to build altitude. He wanted to hedge-hop into the field unobserved, for he was afraid now as he had not been before. He sat frowning at his instruments and worrying about Georgia. Jupiter Aircraft usually meant what it said. There was no doubt of that.

Hunched over the control wheel in the tumbled cabin, Cal Bradley was finding out what real fear is; and with each passing light below, the sensation—a sickening void below his belt—grew in intensity. He forgot what he had just passed through, and forgot to revel in the fact that he was still alive.

After what seemed centuries of flying, he heard himself gunning the engines over the field, and then the sudden shock of the answering landing lights made him realize that he had arrived.

The entire port was thrown into brilliant relief by the monstrous searchlights at its edges. Cal headed in without fishtailing, and placed three points down on the concrete runway. He taxied rapidly toward the hangars, one thought uppermost in his mind. He would get to a phone as quickly as possible and tell Speed Kyle to send Georgia away, out of danger. He would—

A short figure with a limp was coming out to meet him. When Cal stopped the plane, the man shouted at him.

Cal sprang down, not realizing that the ground was cold against his stockinged feet, and saw that the figure was Speed Kyle.

"That you, Cal?" Speed shouted. "Where have you been? I came down to see if you were all right, and—"

Cal's eyes were like javelins as they bored into Speed. "Where's Georgia?" he snapped.

"Why," said Speed, "I left her at the hotel, of course. No need to drag her out just because I was worried. What's the matter?"

58

"She's alone?"

"Sure," said Speed, defensively.

"I guess . . . I guess it won't do any good to—" Cal started for Speed's car at a run. "Come on! We may get there in time, after all!"

CHAPTER SIX

The Clue

ACTIVITY filled the morning sunlight. Motors rumbled high overhead and wings flickered as planes went through complicated maneuvers. The loudspeakers droned on and on, announcing this event and that, lauding this pilot and razzing another. The crowd listened and watched, sighed and cheered, from the overflowing stands. Planes, planes, planes. They stood in three-deep rows back of the lines. They drowned out speech and racked the eardrums. Records were being gained and lost. Some pilots rose to stardom; others flickered out into oblivion. Aviation was in the making.

But around the Kyle hangar all activity had a subdued undertone of worry. The mechanics who swarmed over the big eight-passenger, twin-motored monoplane had little to say to each other or to the two men who stood restlessly in the shade of a wing.

Speed Kyle had aged a dozen years overnight, and Cal Bradley showed what worry and lack of sleep can do even to youth. Nevertheless, his high laced boots were shining, his leather jacket was fresh and his striped helmet was polished. He had found some solace in turning himself out like a gentleman that morning, with some idea that clean clothes would rest him. He had been driving throughout the small hours of the morning—from police station to hotel, from the field to the river, searching for some clue that would lead to Georgia.

They had found her room empty, her clothes gone. An upset chair and a ransacked closet told of violence, and a stricken-eyed elevator operator had been unable to speak, still visualizing the cold, merciless muzzle of the gun that had been shoved into his ribs. The night clerk had been left unconscious behind his desk and his story had been incoherent.

"They wouldn't dare do anything," said Cal. "To her, I mean. They'd maybe keep her out of sight for a while, but that's all. Kidnaping for ransom's a hanging offense in this state."

"I'd give my eye teeth for a smart cop," growled Speed, and he grunted when he remembered that the police had almost locked him up for making a similar remark in the station. "I guess those birds thought we were just going around to amuse ourselves."

Cal sighed. "That wasn't it. They were afraid they'd maybe make a false arrest. They've got to look after their own hides, you know."

"Sure. But that's no call for laughing at us when we told them to arrest McNallan. To listen to them, you'd think a guy with a couple grand in his pocket was a saint, just because he had money."

"I guess we presented ourselves wrong, somehow. I got sore myself when they accused us of just trying to get Jupiter Aircraft out of today's race. But I don't think they'd do anything to Georgia."

Speed looked up from under the bushiness of his brows

and growled, "They'd do anything, and don't kid yourself about it. They're safe enough because they know nobody'll do anything until after the meet, and then it'll be too late. If I could only get my hands on McNallan!"

"But you can't," Cal interrupted. "He'll stay out of our path, and so will Gregory. Besides, Speed, doling out black eyes isn't going to win any races or get Georgia back. If we socked either of those jaspers, they'd have the law on us for assault and battery. Then who'd fly the race?"

"Who'll fly it anyway?" Speed growled. "I've got half a mind to—"

"Withdraw? You couldn't do that, Speed. Georgia wouldn't want you to, if she were here to talk and knew the facts of the case. The only thing we can do is to go in there to win."

Speed shrugged wearily. "I don't know."

"It's all we can do," Cal repeated. "If we allowed ourselves to be licked, we'd lose the whole fight. I know you're worried. Lord, man, you aren't the only one!"

"Sorry," said Speed.

A drab-coated messenger was coming toward them, bearing an envelope. Cal took it and watched the boy disappear around a plane.

"Orders?" Speed asked.

Cal hefted it, as though to judge the contents by the weight, and then ripped it open. Two sheets were there, one of them written by hand, the other on a typewriter. When Cal saw the first, his hand shook slightly.

"Georgia!" he breathed, as he read it.

"Georgia! What's she say?"

Cal cleared his throat. "Dear boys: I've been forced to take a trip, but I'm all right for the present. Georgia."

"Hell!" snapped Speed. "They forced her to write that just so we'd know she was all right! Anything else?"

Cal shook his head, his mouth a tight line. He turned the typewritten sheet over in his hands. "They didn't let her say anything we could use for evidence, but maybe—" He stopped and took a short breath, looking up without seeing anything at which he looked. "I guess they've nailed us this time, Speed."

Speed took the sheet away from him and read it quickly, his brows close together, his mouth twitching at the corners. It read:

Bradley:
If you win today, you'll regret it. We've got the Kyle girl where you won't find her in a thousand years. If you lose, she'll be back with you. If you win, she'll lose her looks. Get it? We're keeping acid handy until we find out how well you take a hint.

Speed said nothing when he finished. He merely looked at Cal with eyes both horrified and pleading.

"They wouldn't!" Cal gritted, but he knew that they would. If he won, Georgia would come back with her face burned. Blind, perhaps. Before Cal's eyes arose the vision of her loveliness—her pointed ivory face, delicate and beautiful.

"You can't do that to her!" Speed muttered. "The contract isn't worth it. Nothing's worth anything beside Georgia's happiness."

Cal brought himself back enough to realize that Speed Kyle had said "you," instead of "we." The decision, then, rested with Cal. . . .

Out in the field, the starter was clearing the sky for the race, and the announcer was telling the crowd all the unusual points of the contest. Even above the dinning engines, Cal could hear the loudspeakers.

"This race," bellowed the huge black maws, "is a contest among four well-known aircraft companies. The ships used will be twin-motored transport planes designed for speed, and carrying the average load for which they will be used. There's a rumor, folks, that the outfits are out for more than the prize money. Up there in the stands with you are officials of one of our biggest transport lines, and, believe me, they're going to watch like hawks. This is a five-lap race around a thirty-five mile course. The time should be a little less than an hour. Performance is the thing. And when the four ships tear down the finishing stretch, we'll know who the big builders of tomorrow will be."

Cal listened, more than a little dazed, his heart sick within him. Under any other conditions those words would have filled him with the fire that always raced in his blood just before the strife. He'd be a little nervous with excitement, and he'd be running his hands over the ship he was to fly, as though he could coax it to do its best. But now he merely plodded up to the ship's belly and stepped inside.

"She's fine as silk!" said Shorty, the chief mechanic. "Feel all right, Cal?"

"Sure. I feel—fit."

"I couldn't get you a cup of coffee or anything?" Shorty persisted. "You look sort of sick, what with being up all night."

"No, I don't want anything," Cal said.

65

"You're not going to pull your throttle or anything, are you?"

Cal didn't look Shorty in the eye. He gazed abstractedly at the instruments, without learning a thing from their faces. Shorty bit his lip and stepped down.

"Don't get sore," said the mechanic. "But I guess—"

"You don't have to ride with me," Cal snapped suddenly. "I'll ride her alone. Throw in an extra sandbag and get the hell out!"

Speed stood in the shadow of an idling motor, looking in. "You won't—?"

"No!" said Cal savagely.

"I couldn't stand it if you did," said Speed, dully. "She's all I've got, Cal. She wouldn't want us to pull our punch, but—"

"I know," Cal said. And he gunned the engines with sudden, vicious stabs that made the dust whip away toward the tail.

Speed stumbled out of the blast and wandered back toward the darkness of the hangar. Then he saw a sudden commotion in the group of mechanics near the door. Speed stopped, his jaw slack, his hands sagging at his sides.

A battered apparition was trotting toward him. A man whose clothes were ripped and muddy, but who bore, nevertheless, the unmistakable stamp of a pilot.

"Bill!" roared Speed. "Bill Conklin!"

"Bill himself," said the apparition, coming to a stop, grinning. "I had the devil's own time doing it, but I got back. I was afraid something would happen to Cal, and you wouldn't have a pilot to run this race for you."

But Speed's sudden exaltation faded and he seemed to shrivel. He gave Bill a pat on the shoulder, and stumbled on toward the hangar door.

Bill Conklin looked after him for a moment and shrugged. He saw the ship ready to go and headed for it at a run, puzzled.

Cal glanced wearily out of the corner of his eye as he saw the shadow appear in the entrance, and then he looked away. Suddenly something seemed to jar inside him and he stared again.

"Bill!" he breathed. "We thought—"

Conklin jumped up into the copilot's seat, grinning once more. "You thought I was dead, I guess. A couple of bruisers threw me into the river. I came to just in time to swim out to a log raft. They pulled me aboard, but—" He paused long enough to chuckle. "They wouldn't believe I had to get back, Cal, and I didn't have any money to make them believe me. I floated with 'em for a day before I could get off. And then one of them lent me enough to grab a rattler back here. Got a smoke?"

Cal handed him a pack of cigarettes and struck a match for him. Bill took a deep, satisfying drag and settled himself in the copilot's seat, buckling his safety belt.

"Guess this is going to be a rough ride," he chortled. "And I'm here to tell you I want to see Jupiter Aircraft whipped right straight off the map!"

Cal compressed his lips. "You're riding the losing ship, Bill."

"G'wan, you're nuts."

"No, I'm not. McNallan's done everything he could think of to keep us out of this race. Last night they got Georgia."

"Georgia! Good Lord, they can't get away with that!"

Cal shrugged and handed over the note Georgia had sent. Bill took it and read the two lines written there, and then he sat back and thought for many seconds.

"No clues?" he said finally.

"None. If we win this race, they threatened to disfigure her." A shudder went over Cal as he said it, and then he plunged on. "There's no way out, Bill. I thought maybe they were bluffing, but I don't think so now."

Bill stared at the letter again, holding it first on one side and then on the other. "She might have left some kind of—look here, Cal—what are these marks?"

Cal leaned forward eagerly. "Thumbnail prints!"

"Sure. They take well on linen. Look here when I hold it so it shines."

Cal took the sheet and looked at it, frowning, hope struggling against despair.

"Three triangles—a dotted line—a square—and a cross," he said, frowning harder.

"The dotted line runs around the three triangles and right past the square," Bill said excitedly. "She made a map of where they took her!"

Cal was looking for writing, but he found none. It was hard enough to read the marks without making out words. For a few seconds his eyes flamed, then they went dead again.

"Too long a shot to risk," he sighed. "We haven't got any chance of finding out what it means, and if we missed fire, we'd be right back where we were before."

"You're right. Too long a shot. Oh, well, it won't be the first time I've ridden the losing ship. Gun her, Cal—the starter's waving a green flag at you."

CHAPTER SEVEN

The Closed Gap

THE green monster which throbbed on their right was a Jupiter ship, and from his pilot's seat, Cal could look across Bill into the furtive face of Smoke Gregory. Now and then the Jupiter pilot glanced up, but quickly averted his eyes.

"He's yellow," Bill decided. "If we didn't have to pull the throttle, we could whip him easy, Cal. This is a better crate any day than that green grasshopper."

Cal nodded glumly and looked again at the starter out in the white ring. The flag whipped down and the Skybird plane seemed to jump away from its shadow, almost immediately soaring upward.

"One off," said Bill.

The green flag came down again in a shimmering arc and the Eaglehawk got away with a blasting drone.

"Jupiter next," Bill muttered.

The third slash of the flag seemed to pull the green monster inside out. Smoke Gregory jammed on the coal and smashed away from the line.

"Give it to 'em!" said Bill.

Fourth and last, the Kyle ship roared away, and hurdling the starter, seemed to quiver with the anticipation of contest. But Cal's left hand on the throttles stopped before the twin levers reached three-quarters of the way along the steel arc. Bill sighed and looked back at the packed grandstands.

"Don't let 'em get too far ahead," he cautioned.

"No! We can't run any risks of winning. Our only chance is to have Smoke crack up." Cal's voice was savage.

"Why don't you fix him? He certainly made hash out of your racer, the first day of the meet."

"I don't fly that way," Cal said. "I never have, and I'm not going to start now. As Speed says, we've got to keep this thing clean."

"McNallan sure isn't straining himself any," Bill snorted.

"What of it? He'll get his in the long run. And he'll get it right between the eyes!"

The Kyle monoplane flashed down toward Pylon One, a little over a hundred yards behind the green monster. Cal kept his throttles as far back as he safely could, but the Jupiter ship did not seem to draw away.

"Damn!" he snapped. "This crate's raring to go, and I've got to hold her in. We aren't doing a hundred and sixty!"

"Right. It's a lot faster than that grasshopper up there. If you gave him a lap, you could still beat him. Look out, Cal."

The caution was directed at the throttles, which the pilot had unconsciously eased ahead. Love of speed was too deeply imbedded in Cal Bradley's makeup to allow him to pull his punch.

With a grunt of disgust, he eased back on the guns and began to synchronize his motors so that their revs would be equal. Scowling at the two tachometers, Cal sagged back and flew automatically.

"Want me to take her?" asked Bill.

Cal shook his head, and eased the ship around Pylon One at a snail's pace. Watching the green plane ahead, he saw it overtake the second ship in line just before they rounded Pylon Two.

"I'm going to take second, anyway," Cal grated. "No use letting those two others shove in their nose."

Roaring back toward the field and the starting line again, Cal let the transport plane out a notch and slid by the Eaglehawk as easily as though that mighty ship stood still. The sight of it did not improve Cal's temper.

"I feel I'm hog-tied!" he snarled.

"Look out, you'll step on Gregory's heels!"

"If he doesn't fly better than that, I'll just have to keep in the air."

The four transport ships swung in single file around the grandstands, their size making them seem to crawl, although in reality they were exceeding the present transport record. It was not a small thing to hurl tons of plane through the air at almost three miles a minute. The eight engines bludgeoned the field for an instant, then the line swung out toward the first pylon again.

Cal slumped down in his seat and flew listlessly. It was galling having to slacken up every time he headed out toward first place. The Kyle ship's performance was so far superior to that of any other plane in the race that it could beat with throttles at three-quarters.

Gregory streaked out to pass the Skybird, passed it without any undue effort. Cal watched him, then swung past the first plane in and to the starting line himself. Each time he looked at his pulled throttles he swore and glowered at the green monoplane ahead. Bill spent most of his time looking down as though the sight of the Jupiter ship sickened him.

"Stop worrying, Cal! If you lose, Georgia'll be all right."

Cal groaned. "Sure, but how about Speed? He'll be handing his identification disk into the poorhouse." The thought of it made him pull back to a safe distance.

They lanced around the field pylon once more to begin lap three. Cal shook his wheel with tight hands.

"Take it, Bill! I'm going crazy hanging onto this thing!"

Bill nodded in understanding. He could feel the tension in Cal's body, and he could experience some of it himself. He pulled the mahogany circle toward himself and began to fly.

Between Pylon Two and Pylon Three, Cal looked down at the countryside, his eyes listless, his chin resting on his left wrist over the window edge. And then he sat up straight, with a sharp exclamation on his lips.

"What's up?" Bill said.

Cal didn't answer. He fumbled in his pocket for Georgia's note, and held it up so that the light was reflected by it.

"See anything?" Bill persisted.

"Look over here!" ordered Cal. "I'll take her."

Bill looked down on Cal's side. "I don't see anything but a big car."

"That's it," said Cal, hoarsely. "That's it! See the chromium fittings above its windshield?"

"Yes."

"Well, I landed on that thing in a chute the other day—and it picked up Gregory when he dropped out last night."

"What are you talking about?"

Cal grinned for the first time that day. "Plenty. See that brick house almost hidden in the trees beside the car? Well, that's what the cross and dotted line meant."

Bill swore with satisfaction. "She made triangles for pylons, and the dotted line for the course. And that place is between Pylon Two and Three. I get it. That's the map!"

"Sure it is! That's where they've got Georgia!"

"Well, I'll be . . . !" Bill muttered.

Exultantly Cal darted off the course and headed down toward the structure, guns all the way on. . . .

The monoplane shivered under the increased speed of motors and dive. The brick house showed up over the nose, growing larger every instant.

Cal looked down when they were but a little more than fifty feet above it. There, in the doorway, a red-faced man hurriedly ducked out of sight.

The control wheel came back and turned, and the plane zoomed sharply back to its course. Ahead, the green monster was growing smaller.

"One lap left!" exclaimed Cal. "That's where they've got her, all right. I know that bird down there."

"And don't *I*, though!" snapped Bill. "He's the one that knocked me for a loop! Pour on the coal, old son—I think we can make it if we try!"

"If they only keep her there until this race is over!" Cal groaned.

"Gee, you shouldn't have gone over like that—they'll move her sure!"

Cal's lips were tight. He crouched over the panel, flying with every nerve in his body taut.

"Have to chance that," he grated.

The field was coming into sight again and under the stress of increased speed the transport plane seemed to knife through the air like a red sword. The green plane had already rounded the home pylon and was proceeding full gun up the first stretch of the last lap.

"There's Speed!" cried Bill. "He's waving at you to slow down."

"Let him worry!" And Cal whipped the monoplane around the home pylon with a smooth swiftness which made the jury struts scream like banshees.

The air bumps they hit made the plane slam and crunch around them, much like a fast boat over high waves. The throttles were in their final notch, and the unsynchronized motors bellowed out in rivalry. The stick and wheel writhed and twisted.

"Hundred and ninety!" shouted Bill. "She's beating her trial record!"

"It isn't fast enough!" cried Cal. "Thicken that mixture, will you?"

Pylon One was racing at them, a swaying, checkered tower. Cal put the huge plane into a vertical so tight that he felt the blood going away from his head.

"Two hundred!" shouted Bill. "Give it to 'em, Cal! Get out of the road, you grasshopper!"

But the Jupiter ship was still some distance ahead, and Cal crouched lower and lower, till he seemed to jackknife into himself.

"That car still there?" he yelled.

"Still put, but there's somebody in it. Look! They're loading the thing up with stuff!"

Cal spared an instant to glance down, and in that instant he saw a white face staring up at him. Georgia? He saw her sling, and waved assurance to her.

"They'll get away!" Bill snapped.

"Have to risk that—we've got a race on our hands."

Bill nodded.

The red transport ship leaped out two hundred feet over the grass tops and began to close in the distance between the Jupiter plane and itself. The motors howled their loudest, and the wings shook at the force of the bumps, but Cal rode hard and fast.

Pylon Three swished by, hardly more than an impression of black and orange checkers. The red plane straightened out with a jerk and lanced down toward the home pylon and the field.

With each passing second, the wires on the tail surfaces of the Jupiter ship grew more distinct. Through the rear port, the black hood of Gregory was visible. Occasionally the hood flashed—Gregory's goggles as he turned to look back.

"Give it to 'em!" Bill exulted. "You've got him now!"

Almost—but not quite. The home pylon reared up like a

sentinel, backed by the dark block which was the crowd. The hangars grew large. The starter held up his flag, ready to tag the winner. Far behind, the Eaglehawk and the Skybird were lumbering, fighting for third place.

The red wing tip of the Kyle plane was even with the Jupiter's tail, but that was not enough. Even though position would win him the race, Cal was determined to push all the way through. The wing tip crept up abreast of the Jupiter's cabin, up beside the green-cowled motors. And then even the crowd on the ground could see that the Kyle ship led by half a length.

The starter's flag swept down, the loudspeakers bellowed and Cal dipped to the stands.

"Made it!" shouted Bill.

Cal nodded, with a tight smile. He cut his guns and banked sharply, coming in to touch his wheels. Three points down, and he braked.

Speed Kyle came up to them in a limping run, his face lined with anxiety. When he saw the grins of his two pilots, he glanced from one to the other, puzzled.

Bill threw a sandbag passenger out to the ground.

"Jump in!" Cal ordered. "We found her!"

"Georgia? You mean it?" Speed cried.

"If we get there in time, it'll be all right." And Cal pulled Speed Kyle into the ship by the nape of the neck. Speed slumped into a wicker chair, still not quite at ease.

Officials were boiling out of the box, watches in hand, faces stern, sweat on their brows.

"Hey, there, Kyle!" someone bawled.

"Be back in fifteen minutes!" Cal shouted above the drumming engines. "Hold everything!"

Cal looked up. The skyways were momentarily clear overhead.

"Let's go!" said Bill.

And Cal gunned the motors, hurdling the Jupiter plane, which was just landing, hoping that Gregory would fail to guess what was taking place. . . .

CHAPTER EIGHT

Retribution

THE countryside was flat and even, save for the silver jags which marked the meandering river; but the distance between Pylon Two and Pylon Three was just a little less than nine miles—and even in the air, nine ground miles is a long distance.

Cal Bradley flew in a beeline toward the brick structure at the side of the course. They had not had time to mark the roadways before, and now, drilling two thousand feet up, they subjected the countryside to a minute study.

"You're sure it was Georgia?" said Speed. "What was their idea of bringing her so close to the course?"

"So Jupiter could keep an eye on them during the race," Bill said. "Maybe they were afraid the rats would try something on their own hook."

Cal opened the window at his elbow and leaned out into the roaring slipstream, looking down. He drew back his head. "How many roads do you see, Bill?"

"Just one. North and south. Asphalt."

"Hmmmm. Do you suppose they'd head for the Canadian border?"

Speed thrust his shaggy head in between the two control seats, close to his pilots' shoulders. "Make up your mind.

If you don't watch out, we'll lose them. This is no time for long-winded parleying!"

"Keep your shirt on," said Cal. "I'm going to try the border theory. They'd have only about two hundred miles to go, but we can do that in an hour."

"Do it, then!" Speed snapped.

Cal whipped the plane into a steep bank and headed north, letting out the throttles until the engines chattered and shook under the wings. He began to descend, coming down above the road, where the speed would be greater and the visibility better. All eyes were on the checkered green fields and the purplish highway.

"They couldn't have gone far," Bill commented. "And they didn't have any reason to turn off on the dirt."

Cal nodded, watching the air speed indicators and the altimeter. Heat-lift from the road was making the air rutty. "Watch under the trees—they may try to hide."

"Watching," said Speed. "When I get my paws on those yellow pups, I'll clean up a lot of territory."

The red plane bored north, making the ground shake with the smashing snarl of its over-revved motors. Houses, stores, creeks, graveyards and woods fled by, blurred with motion. The asphalt stretched out toward the Canadian border like an unending snake.

And then Bill swatted Cal on the shoulder. "There's a big car! Look, there's a car with silver on it!"

Cal nodded again and began to eye the road far ahead. He glanced once at the vehicle below and that was enough. The car was swaying from side to side under the stress of great speed, but the red javelin lanced over and passed it as though it stood quite still.

"Gimme a chute!" Speed demanded. "I'll drop!"

"Forget it!" Bill snapped. "We have no chutes!"

"But what the hell are you—?"

"Wait and see!"

The road was narrow and twisting along this stretch, and Cal fixed his eye on a section which was not cluttered with telegraph wires.

"Can they turn?" he asked.

Bill appraised the situation. "No. The ditches are too close together."

"Fine!" And Cal streaked far ahead of the car, then snapped the red ship into a vertical bank. He worked his rudders to kill excess velocity, and then headed in, pointing toward the road.

"Crosswind," said Bill, unperturbed. "Judge it to the left. No cars for miles, except that one."

Cal pulled his throttles all the way back and began the ticklish task of setting a mighty ship down on a runway too small for a single-seater to land upon.

"Easy!" cautioned Bill. "You're drifting!"

Cal did it easy. He allowed for drift with a micrometer eye, and felt for the asphalt with his wheels. The big ship floated for an instant, and then crunched down exactly in the center of the thoroughfare, wings overhanging well into the field, a ditch close on either side of the fuselage.

Speed grunted. "Good! Let me out!"

Cal set his brakes and sprang to the ground, heading immediately for the left side of the road and a clump of shrubs.

"Here they come!" cried Bill, puffing in Cal's wake.

Cal flung himself down in a crouching position. "Get out of sight!"

Speed, on the other side, hid himself with astonishing swiftness.

The big flashing car slowed down with screaming brakes, swaying as it came to a stop. Its driver, the pinch-faced Tony, stared wide-eyed at the obstruction.

"Turn around!" snapped his red-faced companion.

"Can't!" Tony whined.

The other shot a hand under his coat and whipped out a blue automatic, crouching behind the seat. "Come out of there!" he bawled at the plane.

But there was no sign of life about the red transport. It stood like a wall, its props turning slowly, its engines coughing.

"Come out or I'll shoot!" the red face shouted.

Cal, peering between thorns, grinned to himself, and his grin widened when he saw Georgia. She sat very still on the back seat, looking at the ship with wide, incredulous eyes.

"Take your rod and go up there, Tony!"

"Why me?"

The red-faced gangster swore. "I'll cover you. Get going!"

Tony glanced at the gun, then drew out his own. Cautiously he slid out of the driver's seat and began to creep toward the empty ship, glancing back nervously at every other step.

Out of sight on the other side of the road, Speed shouted, "Drop that gun! I've got you covered!"

Tony whirled, his finger twitching on the trigger, his eyes wide with fear.

"I'll give you three to drop it!" cried Speed. "One . . . two . . ."

And the gun fell from Tony's elevated hands. In the car the red-faced man crouched lower, his back toward one ditch, and tried to find a target for his own weapon.

Cal silently stood up and began to move quietly toward the car. Georgia saw him. Her mouth opened, but no sound came. She understood.

Walking like a cat, Cal reached the running board and started to put his arm through the open window. The buttons on his sleeve rasped suddenly against the metal, and the beefy one whirled and threw up his gun. Cal dodged an instant before a ribbon of flame lashed at him. The bullet whined away from the car.

And then Bill's tousled head and round face came into sight on the opposite side. His short arms stabbed through the door and caught the beefy one by the coat collar. Without waiting to see more, Cal leaped and snatched the uptilted gun. The metal blurred, and then the muzzle was boring into the gangster's soiled vest.

Georgia reached slowly forward and touched Cal's arm, as though to assure herself that he was real, and that all this was not just another hideous nightmare. She smiled and Cal grinned back.

"Okay, Tony," said Cal. "You can step away from that cap pistol—but don't forget to keep your hands where they belong."

Tony, his face twitching, watched with amazement as the

weaponless Speed came out of the brush and retrieved the dropped automatic.

Cal, grinning from ear to ear, lifted Georgia from the seat and deposited her on the asphalt.

"Madame," he said, "your chariot waits. And as for you," Cal said to the gangster, "are you going to talk, or shall I just bore you right here?"

"You're not scaring me any, wise guy. You wouldn't risk boring me. And just for your own good, you better savvy right now that I'm not going to squeal on anybody."

"There's the plane," said Cal. "So step out, while we run this hack off the road."

Bill rolled the shining vehicle from the plane's path and left it in the ditch. And then he came forward to lend Speed moral support in herding the two gangsters into the plane. But Speed needed no such support. He made the others' ribs sore with jabbing, and though Speed's mouth was savage, his old eyes sparkled with joy and satisfaction. He made them sit at the back of the cabin and he sat across the aisle from Georgia, reaching out every few seconds to touch her hand, hardly able to believe she was safe again.

"Let's go," said Bill.

"Gone!" Cal grinned, and the red plane rolled along the asphalt, gathering speed until the wheels lightened and it sprang into the air. Cal smiled back at the girl and took up the task of piloting the plane to the field.

"Only one thing," said Bill in an undertone. "How are we going to get a confession out of these babies? Shall I threaten to throw 'em out at ten thousand?"

"And as for you," Cal said to the gangster, "are you going to talk, or shall I just bore you right here?"

"No," Cal said. "I've a better idea."

"Going to beat 'em up? If they don't talk, we'll have the devil's own time getting anything on McNallan—and we *might* be in some hot water ourselves."

But Cal was too pleased to allow such a minor detail to worry him. Georgia was riding in back of him, and they had won the transport race. He was quite content to let things take care of themselves.

From time to time, Speed growled ferociously at his captives and gestured with the gun, but they took little heed. Tony sat with his head dropped, studying the carpet, and the red-faced gangster tried to take an interest in the countryside.

Ahead, the airport and the stands came into being and gathered distinctness. Another event was in progress, and the planes were stringing out along the first stretch, motors roaring in a dozen different keys. Cal circled lazily, waiting for the end of the affair, when the starter would let him land.

And then the race was over and the crowd was cheering someone. The red ship's wheels crunched on the concrete, ground looping, to taxi over in front of the judges' box and the stands.

One of the officials scrambled down the steps and approached the fuselage. "What the hell was the idea—" He caught sight of Georgia. "Sorry, ma'am. I mean, why'd you run off like that? The Amalgamated crowd are chewing their fingernails, and a couple of Brazilians have been driving us nutty with their chatter."

"Business," said Cal. "Business. All out—this is the end of the line."

Speed thrust the automatic into his pocket. "Get down, you pups, and if you try to run I'll blast you for the record!"

The two mobsters climbed down, standing circumspectly, and looking over at the line where the Jupiter ship was ticking over, seemingly ready to take off. Cal signaled and Bill slipped quietly away.

Cal stepped in between the two captives and walked them up the steps of the judges' stand.

"So you aren't a squealer," said Cal.

"No," snapped the man with the red face. "I'm not and never will be."

"And *you* don't want to talk to save your own neck?"

"Naw," rasped Tony.

"If you don't, McNallan and Gregory'll get away," Cal said.

The red-faced gangster laughed. "You can't pin anything on me." He glanced around to see that no one stood within hearing distance of his low tones. "McNallan and Gregory paid me plenty. I got enough to hire a mouthpiece and get clear, and if this Jupiter Aircraft gang sticks around, I'll be able to wheedle plenty of jack out of them for this day's work."

Cal shrugged. "So you'd blackmail them. That it?"

"Sure, why not? After all, I'm not risking my neck for nothing, and if I squealed on them now—well you know how it is."

"Sure, I know," said Cal. "And you're perfectly willing to admit the abduction of Miss Kyle and the attempted murder of Bill Conklin?"

"Who said anything about admitting it? I'm not talking until I get a mouthpiece. What're you so sore about? This

Conklin bird's alive, ain't he? And you got the girl back, didn't you?"

"That wasn't your fault, though," Cal sighed. "Why confess to me that you did it?"

"Because your word won't amount to a hill of beans, see? You haven't got any witnesses, and you can't get any."

Cal's mouth widened in a huge grin. "Swell! How would you like to know that you've got twenty thousand people listening to you?"

The gangster snorted in derision, and then his eye happened to light on a little black box which stood just behind them. His jaw slacked and his squinted eyes traveled up the wires to the poles which held the microphones.

"Cripes!" Tony whined. "You lummox! You've been blabbing the works to the crowd!"

The two gangsters wilted in their tracks. Their eyes went away from the rows of laughing people and sought the rough planks of the platform.

And then from the edge of the stands two men leaped over the railing and sped toward the Jupiter plane.

"Look out!" shouted Speed. "It's McNallan and Gregory!" He started to run, but Cal called him back.

"Wait, Speed!"

The head of Jupiter Aircraft and his chief pilot dashed around a wing and leaped for the door handle, but, unaccountably, the door swung open in their faces and a pistol muzzle bore upon them.

"Going someplace?" Bill Conklin inquired with a grin.

Smoke Gregory and McNallan stopped, arms raised, their

faces frozen with surprise. And then, without a word, they led the way back to the judges' and announcer's stand.

Three members of the state police met them at the bottom of the stairs and took them in hand.

"I don't quite get this," said a sergeant, "but it sounds bad, anyhow. Let's have those two birds that squawked through the mikes."

Cal shoved the mobsters down toward the waiting handcuffs. Speed chuckled.

"Well, McNallan!" he said. "I told you we had to keep this game clean. It's not like the old auto racing days any more."

But McNallan's eyes were on the ground as the four were led away.

And then someone was jabbering in broken English at Speed's side.

"The altitude test—we have just heard. It is supreme, it is marvelous!"

"Huh?" Speed grunted, taken by surprise.

"I said the altitude test, she was wonderful!" continued the dapper, olive-faced man. "Will you sign a contract now, or do you wish to sign later?"

But before Speed could answer, a bluff, hearty voice hailed him from the railing:

"Hello, Kyle! Come on over to our hangars and we'll sign everything at once."

Speed blinked, then recognized the head of Amalgamated Airlines. He blinked again. "Sure, we'll sign everything at once," he said. "But maybe you'd like to see the plane first. Up close, I mean."

"Hell, I've been looking at it for the last ten minutes, and we timed your last lap! Let's go!"

Speed hung back for an instant, waiting for Cal to turn, but Cal didn't look up and Speed went on alone.

Cal had quite enough to hold his attention at that minute. Georgia was there, radiant.

"Let's not worry about that contract now," Cal said. "Tomorrow's another day. We'll pull out for the factory early in the morning and I'll get things in hand."

"But," said Georgia, "tomorrow's the last day of the meet and there's a high-speed race on the bill."

"What of it? You said three hundred miles an hour was too fast for anybody."

"I was wrong," said Georgia. "I think it's swell. Besides, you've never flown Dad's fastest ship, and I think you ought to get all the glory you deserve. So far, you haven't done anything but worry in this meet. It's time you amused yourself."

Cal Bradley stood and looked down at her, his eyes bright. "Mean it?" he said.

"Surest thing in the world. And you're a winner, Cal."

Georgia's eyes were dancing. She seemed utterly content.

"Boy!" Cal breathed. "What a day tomorrow will be!"

Story Preview

N OW that you've just ventured through one of the captivating tales in the Stories from the Golden Age collection by L. Ron Hubbard, turn the page and enjoy a preview of *On Blazing Wings*. Join David Duane, artist, adventurer and air ace, who discovers his destiny awaiting him inside a mystery-shrouded Finnish city of golden minarets. As Duane bravely confronts and challenges his fate, the action swirls to an explosive climax amidst a fierce aerial dogfight with an unexpected toll.

On Blazing Wings

IN the black crystal of a Lapland night, men spoke in whispers while they awaited the coming of dawn and battle. Squadron Three of the Second Regiment of the *Ilmavoimat, Lentorykmentti,* complained like sleepy eagles upon the line, their Mercury VIIs clanking and wheezing, dying out and revving up as though suddenly emerging from a nap into instant awareness of their responsibilities that day.

It was becoming barely possible at this hour of 9:00 AM to make out the Fokker D.XXIs which spread their wings close against the breast of earth, shadows against the weirdly beautiful luminescence of the snow.

Overhead the brilliance of the northern lights faded slowly before the coming of a briefly interested sun. In the north, the Wind Mother had already stilled her charges. Day was being ushered in—the most important day in the life of David Duane.

The pilots huddled about an oil fire in an odorous *choom,* pretending to find heat in it, but quite able to see one another's breath, and all continually flexing their ungloved hands to keep the frost from creeping in. By the smoky light of the oil lantern, hanging from a wooden hook on a pole which reached across the upper half of the skin tent, these men looked like Arctic bears with human masks; their *militzkas* were huge and shaggy, and bulging because of the flying suits underneath; their legs, encased in stumplike *pimmies,* enhanced the impression. They were not dressed in accordance with Finn regulations, for each had his own idea on how to keep warm. Besides, could they not allow themselves a liberty in many things, considering their post here?

The Russians were less than thirty kilometers to the east, and the Russians were persistent in advancing to suicide upon the daggers and into the bullets of the stubbornly resisting handful of Finns. And supporting these valiant troops in white was Squadron Three.

If gas could be gotten, if bullets and bombs and engine parts came up, then Squadron Three could continue to carry on. But gas, so far north, was dear, and bullets and bombs were few. For not much weight can be carried by air transport, especially when nearly all available planes were battling bitterly in the south with an enemy of tremendous superiority in the air as well as on the ground; and on those days when planes could be had, then the weather was too bad and the transport pilots must brave the danger of missing this hastily organized port and flying far out into the Arctic Sea to be lost in the eerie flare of the northern lights.

It was a suicide post, just as it was a suicide war. Not one man in this group really expected to come out alive. Shot down behind Russian lines, a pilot became a prey to furious troops—if he did not freeze.

"I do not think it is so," said a young Finn lieutenant. "I think it is something which gets into a man's head—a premonition which takes the form of a vision."

"Saj saw no vision," replied David Duane's right wingman. "What he saw was a mirage—like the city Galahad saw when he parted from Sir Percivale and mounted up into the sky."

"I think it was a vision," said the lieutenant. "Three men have seen it now, and those three are gone. Saj saw it, and Saj is gone. Why haven't the rest of us seen it? Why haven't I seen it—I who led his flight?"

"Perhaps," said David, "you are to be with us yet awhile, our machine-gun sweetheart."

"And perhaps not," said the lieutenant with a shrug. "But I still say—"

"It's a mirage," said the right wingman. "Though I can't claim any such travels as our pet wolf David, still I have seen a thing or two. And once, in the Arctic, I saw a mirage of a town. It *must* have been a mirage, because everyone else saw it as well."

"You defeat yourself," said the lieutenant. "The rest of us do not see this mirage, and those who *have* seen it have not been with us more than a week or two thereafter. I'm not superstitious, but if I see it, I'm quite sure I shall make a will and pass out from sheer fright."

"No doubt," said David ironically. "And take half a dozen of the Red gentlemen along with you to ply you with bromides. There are too many things about this north which are strange to me for me to doubt anything."

"Then don't doubt that it's just a mirage," said the right wingman. "All this nonsense—"

"The Lapps believe in such a city," said a captain. "Or at least they believe in such a land beyond this. Their word for God is also their word for sky—*Jumala*—and they keep speaking of a heaven on top of the hills—*hiisi*. And their *Puhjola* isn't unlike the Norse *Valhalla*. Only those killed in battle can go to *Puhjola*, and our three brothers were very certainly warriors. If they saw *Puhjola*—"

"It's just a mirage," said the right wingman. "Why, there's such a mirage in Alaska. In the winter it appears to be a city built on the clouds, perfect in every detail. Why, it's so real that a pilot in the United States Army flew right into it trying to find out what town it was. And you'll all admit that this country is crazy with mirages. Why, only yesterday I almost pulled my ship apart trying to get away from a flight of our Red friends, only to look back and discover that they hadn't existed, except as reflections on the air. Maybe what I saw was just a picture projected from a real Red flight, perhaps far to the south."

"Saj didn't make any ordinary town of it," said the captain. "He described to me a city which couldn't possibly exist in this day. Golden minarets and domes, parks and wide streets—"

The dull cough and sigh of a rocket shell, their takeoff signal, brought them lumbering from the *choom*. The air was so clear and sharp that their senses were quickened instantly into excitement. The rim of a pale sun was barely showing on the southern horizon, spreading a blue twilight over the limitless table of snow.

David had a feeling of unreality. His *pimmies* crunched on the snow crust—as hard and brittle as rock salt; his goggles were like panes of ice. He mounted to his catwalk and thrust back the cockpit screen, feeling the Fokker rock sturdily under his weight.

"I fixed your motor cannon," said an ordnance officer on the other side of the ship. "I hope it won't jam today."

"Thanks," said David, and the puff of breath which came out with the word was so instantly frozen that it tinkle-tinkled as it dropped on the metal cowl.

David slid into the pit and adjusted the seat a trifle. The ordnance officer dropped the screen. David ran an eye over his instrument panel. The warm air from the engine was welcome upon his face and he went through contortions to remove his *pimmies* and *militzka,* for to sweat in here meant to freeze a little later outside.

As leader of the third flight, he waited for the first to get away. And then, pacing the second, with a wave to his two wingmen, he cracked the throttle. The ship jolted as the skis broke loose and then sped forward with a triumphant snarl.

David Duane had begun the most important day of his life.

To find out more about *On Blazing Wings* and how you can obtain your copy, go to www.goldenagestories.com.

Glossary

STORIES FROM THE GOLDEN AGE *reflect the words and expressions used in the 1930s and 1940s, adding unique flavor and authenticity to the tales. While a character's speech may often reflect regional origins, it also can convey attitudes common in the day. So that readers can better grasp such cultural and historical terms, uncommon words or expressions of the era, the following glossary has been provided.*

ailerons: hinged flaps on the trailing edge of an aircraft wing, used to control banking movements.

altimeter: a gauge that measures altitude.

Andes: a mountain range that extends the length of the western coast of South America.

ballyhoo artist: someone who uses exaggerated or lurid material in order to gain public attention.

banshees: (Irish legend) female spirits whose wailing warns of a death in a house.

barograph: a barometer that automatically records on paper the variations in atmospheric pressure.

Chi: Chicago.

***choom*:** (Lapp) a tent made of skins or bark.

cock-and-bull story: a tale so full of improbable details and embellishments that it is obviously not true.

cowl or **cowling:** the removable metal housing of an aircraft engine, often designed as part of the airplane's body, containing the cockpit, passenger seating and cargo but excluding the wings.

Department of Commerce: the department of the US federal government that promotes and administers domestic and foreign commerce. In 1926, Congress passed an Air Commerce Act that gave the US Department of Commerce some regulation over air facilities, the authority to establish air traffic rules and the authority to issue licenses and certificates.

Duralumin: a strong low-density aluminum alloy used especially in aircraft.

Fokker D.XXI: a fighter plane designed in 1935 and used by the Finnish Air Force in the early years of World War II. Designed as a cheap and small but rugged plane, they were very suitable for the Finnish winter conditions. They performed better and for much longer than other fighter planes acquired prior to the start of the war, and were more evenly matched with the fighter planes of the Soviet Air Force.

Gabriel: the archangel who will blow a sacred trumpet or horn to announce Judgment Day.

Galahad: Sir Galahad; the noblest knight of the Round Table, who succeeded in his quest for the Holy Grail (cup or plate that possessed miraculous powers; according to medieval legend it was used by Jesus at the Last Supper and later became sought by medieval knights). Upon this achievement, he was taken up into heaven, leaving behind two companions and fellow knights who also sought the Holy Grail.

G-men: government men; agents of the Federal Bureau of Investigation.

ground loop: to cause an aircraft to ground loop, or make a sharp horizontal turn when taxiing, landing or taking off.

hook, on his own: by oneself; independently.

Ilmavoimat, Lentorykmentti: (Finnish) a flying regiment in the air force.

jack: money.

jalopies: outdated, often mechanically inferior models (as of airplanes).

jaspers: fellows; guys.

jury strut: a strut that keeps an aircraft's wings from bowing or snapping when air pressure pushes down on them.

lam: to escape or run away, especially from the law.

Lapland: a region of extreme northern Europe including northern Norway, Sweden and Finland and the Kola Peninsula of northwest Russia. It is largely within the Arctic Circle.

mazuma: money.

Mercury VII: type of engine in the Fokker D.XXI plane.

militzka: (Samoyed, the language of the nomadic peoples of northern Siberia) winter coat made of reindeer hide.

monoplane: an airplane with one sustaining surface or one set of wings.

motor cannon: a type of gun that shoots through the propeller hub of a fighter plane.

mouthpiece: a lawyer, especially a criminal lawyer.

NAA: National Aeronautics Association; established in 1922 as a nonprofit organization "dedicated to the advancement of the art, sport and science of aviation in the United States." It is the official record-keeper for US aviation and provides observers and compiles the data necessary to certify aviation and spaceflight records of all kinds.

Percivale, Sir: a knight of the Round Table who sought the Holy Grail (cup or plate that possessed miraculous powers; according to medieval legend it was used by Jesus at the Last Supper and later became sought by medieval knights).

pimmies: (Samoyed, the language of the nomadic peoples of northern Siberia) boots made of deerskin.

prop wash: the disturbed mass of air pushed aft by the propeller of an aircraft.

Puhjola: borrowed from *Pohjola* in Finnish mythology, it means "the home of the north" though the term is quite vague and without geographical significance. It is considered to be the land of heroes.

pylons: towers marking turning points in a race among aircraft.

rattler: a fast freight train.

roadster: an open-top automobile with a single seat in front for two or three persons, a fabric top and either a luggage compartment or a rumble seat in back. A rumble seat is an upholstered exterior seat with a hinged lid that opens to form the back of the seat when in use.

rod: another name for a handgun.

rudder: a device used to steer ships or aircraft. A rudder is a flat plane or sheet of material attached with hinges to the craft's stern or tail. In typical aircraft, pedals operate rudders via mechanical linkages.

Scheherazade: the female narrator of *The Arabian Nights,* who during one thousand and one adventurous nights saved her life by entertaining her husband, the king, with stories.

shrouds: the ropes connecting the harness and canopy of a parachute.

skidded: (of an airplane) moved sideways in a turn because of insufficient banking.

slipstream: the airstream pushed back by a revolving aircraft propeller.

smeared: smashed.

snap rolled: (of an aircraft) quickly rolled about its longitudinal axis while flying horizontally.

spike your guns: to spoil someone's plans. The phrase "spike a gun" comes from rendering a cannon useless by driving a spike into the touchhole where the cannon powder is ignited.

stabilizer: a device that provides aircraft stability and longitudinal balance in flight, using horizontal and vertical stabilizers (fins) that are similar to the aircraft wing in structural design and function of providing lift at an angle to the wind.

stall: a situation in which an aircraft suddenly dives because the airflow is obstructed and lift is lost. The loss of airflow can be caused by insufficient airspeed or by an excessive angle of an airfoil (part of an aircraft's surface that provides lift or control) when the aircraft is climbing.

tachometers: devices used to determine speed of rotation, typically of an engine's crankshaft, usually measured in revolutions per minute.

tarmac: airport runway.

three points: three-point landing; an airplane landing in which the two main wheels and the nose wheel all touch the ground simultaneously.

turtleback: the part of the airplane behind the cockpit that is shaped like the back of a turtle.

Valhalla: (Norse mythology) the great hall where the souls of heroes killed in battle spend eternity.

Wind Mother: (Latvian mythology) Goddess of the Wind. Latvians called all their gods "father" and all their goddesses "mother." They pictured all their deities as parents. Latvia is a country in northern Europe along the shores of the Baltic Sea.

L. Ron Hubbard
in the Golden Age
of Pulp Fiction

*In writing an adventure story
a writer has to know that he is adventuring
for a lot of people who cannot.
The writer has to take them here and there
about the globe and show them
excitement and love and realism.
As long as that writer is living the part of an
adventurer when he is hammering
the keys, he is succeeding with his story.*

*Adventuring is a state of mind.
If you adventure through life, you have a
good chance to be a success on paper.*

*Adventure doesn't mean globe-trotting,
exactly, and it doesn't mean great deeds.
Adventuring is like art.
You have to live it to make it real.*

— *L. RON HUBBARD*

L. Ron Hubbard
and American
Pulp Fiction

B ORN March 13, 1911, L. Ron Hubbard lived a life at least as expansive as the stories with which he enthralled a hundred million readers through a fifty-year career.

Originally hailing from Tilden, Nebraska, he spent his formative years in a classically rugged Montana, replete with the cowpunchers, lawmen and desperadoes who would later people his Wild West adventures. And lest anyone imagine those adventures were drawn from vicarious experience, he was not only breaking broncs at a tender age, he was also among the few whites ever admitted into Blackfoot society as a bona fide blood brother. While if only to round out an otherwise rough and tumble youth, his mother was that rarity of her time—a thoroughly educated woman—who introduced her son to the classics of Occidental literature even before his seventh birthday.

But as any dedicated L. Ron Hubbard reader will attest, his world extended far beyond Montana. In point of fact, and as the son of a United States naval officer, by the age of eighteen he had traveled over a quarter of a million miles. Included therein were three Pacific crossings to a then still mysterious Asia, where he ran with the likes of Her British Majesty's agent-in-place

L. Ron Hubbard,
left, at Congressional
Airport, Washington,
DC, 1931, with
members of George
Washington
University flying
club.

for North China, and the last in the line of Royal Magicians from the court of Kublai Khan. For the record, L. Ron Hubbard was also among the first Westerners to gain admittance to forbidden Tibetan monasteries below Manchuria, and his photographs of China's Great Wall long graced American geography texts.

Upon his return to the United States and a hasty completion of his interrupted high school education, the young Ron Hubbard entered George Washington University. There, as fans of his aerial adventures may have heard, he earned his wings as a pioneering barnstormer at the dawn of American aviation. He also earned a place in free-flight record books for the longest sustained flight above Chicago. Moreover, as a roving reporter for *Sportsman Pilot* (featuring his first professionally penned articles), he further helped inspire a generation of pilots who would take America to world airpower.

Immediately beyond his sophomore year, Ron embarked on the first of his famed ethnological expeditions, initially to then untrammeled Caribbean shores (descriptions of which would later fill a whole series of West Indies mystery-thrillers). That the Puerto Rican interior would also figure into the future of Ron Hubbard stories was likewise no accident. For in addition to cultural studies of the island, a 1932–33

LRH expedition is rightly remembered as conducting the first complete mineralogical survey of a Puerto Rico under United States jurisdiction.

There was many another adventure along this vein: As a lifetime member of the famed Explorers Club, L. Ron Hubbard charted North Pacific waters with the first shipboard radio direction finder, and so pioneered a long-range navigation system universally employed until the late twentieth century. While not to put too fine an edge on it, he also held a rare Master Mariner's license to pilot any vessel, of any tonnage in any ocean.

Yet lest we stray too far afield, there is an LRH note at this juncture in his saga, and it reads in part:

"I started out writing for the pulps, writing the best I knew, writing for every mag on the stands, slanting as well as I could."

To which one might add: His earliest submissions date from the summer of 1934, and included tales drawn from true-to-life Asian adventures, with characters roughly modeled on British/American intelligence operatives he had known in Shanghai. His early Westerns were similarly peppered with details drawn from personal experience. Although therein lay a first hard lesson from the often cruel world of the pulps. His first Westerns were soundly rejected as lacking the authenticity of a Max Brand yarn

Capt. L. Ron Hubbard in Ketchikan, Alaska, 1940, on his Alaskan Radio Experimental Expedition, the first of three voyages conducted under the Explorers Club flag.

(a particularly frustrating comment given L. Ron Hubbard's Westerns came straight from his Montana homeland, while Max Brand was a mediocre New York poet named Frederick Schiller Faust, who turned out implausible six-shooter tales from the terrace of an Italian villa).

Nevertheless, and needless to say, L. Ron Hubbard persevered and soon earned a reputation as among the most publishable names in pulp fiction, with a ninety percent placement rate of first-draft manuscripts. He was also among the most prolific, averaging between seventy and a hundred thousand words a month. Hence the rumors that L. Ron Hubbard had redesigned a typewriter for faster keyboard action and pounded out manuscripts on a continuous roll of butcher paper to save the precious seconds it took to insert a single sheet of paper into manual typewriters of the day.

That all L. Ron Hubbard stories did not run beneath said byline is yet another aspect of pulp fiction lore. That is, as publishers periodically rejected manuscripts from top-drawer authors if only to avoid paying top dollar, L. Ron Hubbard and company just as frequently replied with submissions under various pseudonyms. In Ron's case, the

A MAN OF MANY NAMES

Between 1934 and 1950, L. Ron Hubbard authored more than fifteen million words of fiction in more than two hundred classic publications. To supply his fans and editors with stories across an array of genres and pulp titles, he adopted fifteen pseudonyms in addition to his already renowned L. Ron Hubbard byline.

*Winchester Remington Colt
Lt. Jonathan Daly
Capt. Charles Gordon
Capt. L. Ron Hubbard
Bernard Hubbel
Michael Keith
Rene Lafayette
Legionnaire 148
Legionnaire 14830
Ken Martin
Scott Morgan
Lt. Scott Morgan
Kurt von Rachen
Barry Randolph
Capt. Humbert Reynolds*

list included: Rene Lafayette, Captain Charles Gordon, Lt. Scott Morgan and the notorious Kurt von Rachen—supposedly on the lam for a murder rap, while hammering out two-fisted prose in Argentina. The point: While L. Ron Hubbard as Ken Martin spun stories of Southeast Asian intrigue, LRH as Barry Randolph authored tales of

L. Ron Hubbard, circa 1930, at the outset of a literary career that would finally span half a century.

romance on the Western range—which, stretching between a dozen genres is how he came to stand among the two hundred elite authors providing close to a million tales through the glory days of American Pulp Fiction.

In evidence of exactly that, by 1936 L. Ron Hubbard was literally leading pulp fiction's elite as president of New York's American Fiction Guild. Members included a veritable pulp hall of fame: Lester "Doc Savage" Dent, Walter "The Shadow" Gibson, and the legendary Dashiell Hammett—to cite but a few.

Also in evidence of just where L. Ron Hubbard stood within his first two years on the American pulp circuit: By the spring of 1937, he was ensconced in Hollywood, adopting a Caribbean thriller for Columbia Pictures, remembered today as *The Secret of Treasure Island*. Comprising fifteen thirty-minute episodes, the L. Ron Hubbard screenplay led to the most profitable matinée serial in Hollywood history. In accord with Hollywood culture, he was thereafter continually called upon

The 1937 Secret of Treasure Island, *a fifteen-episode serial adapted for the screen by L. Ron Hubbard from his novel,* Murder at Pirate Castle.

to rewrite/doctor scripts—most famously for long-time friend and fellow adventurer Clark Gable.

In the interim—and herein lies another distinctive chapter of the L. Ron Hubbard story—he continually worked to open Pulp Kingdom gates to up-and-coming authors. Or, for that matter, anyone who wished to write. It was a fairly unconventional stance, as markets were already thin and competition razor sharp. But the fact remains, it was an L. Ron Hubbard hallmark that he vehemently lobbied on behalf of young authors—regularly supplying instructional articles to trade journals, guest-lecturing to short story classes at George Washington University and Harvard, and even founding his own creative writing competition. It was established in 1940, dubbed the Golden Pen, and guaranteed winners both New York representation and publication in *Argosy*.

But it was John W. Campbell Jr.'s *Astounding Science Fiction* that finally proved the most memorable LRH vehicle. While every fan of L. Ron Hubbard's galactic epics undoubtedly knows the story, it nonetheless bears repeating: By late 1938, the pulp publishing magnate of Street & Smith was determined to revamp *Astounding Science Fiction* for broader readership. In particular, senior editorial director F. Orlin Tremaine called for stories with a stronger *human element*. When acting editor John W. Campbell balked, preferring his spaceship-driven tales, Tremaine enlisted Hubbard. Hubbard, in turn, replied with the genre's first truly *character-driven* works, wherein heroes are pitted not against bug-eyed monsters but the mystery and majesty of deep space itself—and thus was launched the Golden Age of Science Fiction.

The names alone are enough to quicken the pulse of any science fiction aficionado, including LRH friend and protégé, Robert Heinlein, Isaac Asimov, A. E. van Vogt and Ray Bradbury. Moreover, when coupled with LRH stories of fantasy, we further come to what's rightly been described as the foundation of every modern tale of horror: L. Ron Hubbard's immortal *Fear.* It was rightly proclaimed by Stephen King as one of the very few works to genuinely warrant that overworked term "classic"—as in: *"This is a classic tale of creeping, surreal menace and horror. . . . This is one of the really, really good ones."*

L. Ron Hubbard, 1948, among fellow science fiction luminaries at the World Science Fiction Convention in Toronto.

To accommodate the greater body of L. Ron Hubbard fantasies, Street & Smith inaugurated *Unknown*—a classic pulp if there ever was one, and wherein readers were soon thrilling to the likes of *Typewriter in the Sky* and *Slaves of Sleep* of which Frederik Pohl would declare: *"There are bits and pieces from Ron's work that became part of the language in ways that very few other writers managed."*

And, indeed, at J. W. Campbell Jr.'s insistence, Ron was regularly drawing on themes from the Arabian Nights and so introducing readers to a world of genies, jinn, Aladdin and Sinbad—all of which, of course, continue to float through cultural mythology to this day.

At least as influential in terms of post-apocalypse stories was L. Ron Hubbard's 1940 *Final Blackout*. Generally acclaimed as the finest anti-war novel of the decade and among the ten best works of the genre ever authored—here, too, was a tale that would live on in ways few other writers imagined.

Portland, Oregon, 1943; L. Ron Hubbard, captain of the US Navy subchaser PC 815.

Hence, the later Robert Heinlein verdict: "Final Blackout *is as perfect a piece of science fiction as has ever been written.*"

Like many another who both lived and wrote American pulp adventure, the war proved a tragic end to Ron's sojourn in the pulps. He served with distinction in four theaters and was highly decorated for commanding corvettes in the North Pacific. He was also grievously wounded in combat, lost many a close friend and colleague and thus resolved to say farewell to pulp fiction and devote himself to what it had supported these many years—namely, his serious research.

But in no way was the LRH literary saga at an end, for as he wrote some thirty years later, in 1980:

"Recently there came a period when I had little to do. This was novel in a life so crammed with busy years, and I decided to amuse myself by writing a novel that was pure *science fiction."*

That work was *Battlefield Earth: A Saga of the Year 3000*. It was an immediate *New York Times* bestseller and, in fact, the first international science fiction blockbuster in decades. It was not, however, L. Ron Hubbard's magnum opus, as that distinction is generally reserved for his next and final work: The 1.2 million word *Mission Earth*.

> **Final Blackout**
> *is as perfect*
> *a piece of*
> *science fiction*
> *as has ever*
> *been written.*
>
> —Robert Heinlein

How he managed those 1.2 million words in just over twelve months is yet another piece of the L. Ron Hubbard legend. But the fact remains, he did indeed author a ten-volume *dekalogy* that lives in publishing history for the fact that each and every volume of the series was also a *New York Times* bestseller.

Moreover, as subsequent generations discovered L. Ron Hubbard through republished works and novelizations of his screenplays, the mere fact of his name on a cover signaled an international bestseller. . . . Until, to date, sales of his works exceed hundreds of millions, and he otherwise remains among the most enduring and widely read authors in literary history. Although as a final word on the tales of L. Ron Hubbard, perhaps it's enough to simply reiterate what editors told readers in the glory days of American Pulp Fiction:

He writes the way he does, brothers, because he's been there, seen it and done it!

THE STORIES FROM THE GOLDEN AGE

Your ticket to adventure starts here with the Stories from the Golden Age collection by master storyteller L. Ron Hubbard. These gripping tales are set in a kaleidoscope of exotic locales and brim with fascinating characters, including some of the most vile villains, dangerous dames and brazen heroes you'll ever get to meet.

The entire collection of over one hundred and fifty stories is being released in a series of eighty books and audiobooks. For an up-to-date listing of available titles, go to www.goldenagestories.com.

AIR ADVENTURE

FAR-FLUNG ADVENTURE

SEA ADVENTURE

TALES FROM THE ORIENT

MYSTERY

119

FANTASY

SCIENCE FICTION

WESTERN

JOIN THE PULP REVIVAL
America in the 1930s and 40s

Pulp fiction was in its heyday and 30 million readers were regularly riveted by the larger-than-life tales of master storyteller L. Ron Hubbard. For this was pulp fiction's golden age, when the writing was raw and every page packed a walloping punch.

That magic can now be yours. An evocative world of nefarious villains, exotic intrigues, courageous heroes and heroines—a world that today's cinema has barely tapped for tales of adventure and swashbucklers.

Enroll today in the Stories from the Golden Age Club and begin receiving your monthly feature edition selected from more than 150 stories in the collection.

You may choose to enjoy them as either a paperback or audiobook for the special membership price of $9.95 each month along with FREE shipping and handling.

CALL TOLL-FREE: 1-877-8GALAXY
(1-877-842-5299) OR GO ONLINE TO
www.goldenagestories.com
AND BECOME PART OF THE PULP REVIVAL!